REVEREND MARGOT QUADE

COZY MYSTERIES BOOKS 4-6

S.E. BIGLOW

MY BROTHER'S KEEPER

A REVEREND MARGOT QUADE
COZY MYSTERY NOVELLA BOOK 4

My Brother's Keeper

S.E. BIGLOW

For information contact; www.sarah-biglow.com

Copyedited by: Liza Street

Proofreading and Formatting by: Under Wraps Publishing Services

Cover Design by: Deranged Doctor Design

Published by Sarah Biglow: May 2020

10 9 8 7 6 5 4 3 2 1

 Created with Vellum

The huff of the bus's hydraulic brakes roused Margot from her doze. She opened her eyes and stared out the bus's window at the snowy mounds covering every available inch of landscape outside of Belvedere's Bed and Breakfast in Collingwood, Vermont. The small town was just a short trip from Port Marie. While Margot loved her hometown, after the year she'd had, she needed a break.

The little B&B would be the perfect getaway for New Year's Eve. Chances were, she'd spend it in the company of strangers, not that she minded. Although, now that she was here, a part of her questioned why she hadn't accepted Sam's offer to spend the holiday together like they'd done in their youth.

"This is where you needed to go, right ma'am?" The driver called out to her when she had stayed rooted to the sidewalk in front of the quaint, three-story house with rosy pink shutters and cream-colored siding.

"Yes, thank you," she answered with a forced smile. Then she closed the distance to the tiny front porch and shouldered her way through the front door into a cozy foyer.

Heat blasted from old-fashioned radiators and she let the warmth seep into her skin, beating back the chill from her brief time outside. Even after having time to acclimate to New England weather, she was convinced her core temperature was stuck in the Middle East.

As she let the heat revive her, Margot

took a moment to take in her surroundings. The house was a typical New England home with wood paneling and tasteful prints of town squares and ocean views leading up the first set of stairs. Directly ahead of her sat a small desk, and off to her left she heard the commotion of people around a dinner table. She left her bag by the front desk and poked her head into the dining room. Six people sat around a heavy oak table.

"Oh, you must be Margot," an older woman with gray hair announced, her voice carrying across the room, loud enough to stop the side conversations.

"Yes, ma'am," Margot answered. "I'm sorry to interrupt dinner. The bus was behind schedule."

"Nonsense, come right in." The woman turned her attention to a teenage girl staring transfixed at her phone. "Valerie, put that thing down and go get another place setting."

Valerie let out a sigh, but set the phone

down and walked past Margot toward what Margot assumed was the kitchen. The woman rounded the table and extended a hand to Margot.

"Caroline Belvedere. Proprietor."

Margot shook Caroline's hand. "It's very nice to meet you."

Caroline glanced over her shoulder at the other diners. "You can take the seat beside Kalina," she said, pointing to a redheaded woman possibly in her early thirties.

Margot took the seat offered to her as Valerie returned with a bowl and utensils. As she served herself some soup and bread, Margot took stock of her fellow boarders. Kalina eyed the man beside her. She noted they both wore wedding rings and it was a likely assumption that they were here together. Despite that connection, Margot caught the averted glances and the tight lines around both of their mouths.

She turned her attention to the pair on

her right. The young man sported a military buzz cut and she spotted dog tags around his neck. He offered her his hand. "Private Dennis Parker."

"Margot Quade, former Army Chaplain." Margot felt the weight of her own dog tags and cross against her chest. They were a comforting reminder of her calling.

The young woman on Dennis' other side sat hunched over her bowl of soup, the sleeves of her turtleneck sweater pulled down well over her hands. Margot thought she saw the faint yellowish green of a healing bruise on her left cheekbone. Her blonde hair fell over one shoulder. The table dropped into an uneasy silence, everyone turning their attention back to the meal.

"So, Dennis, what branch of the military did you say you were in?" Caroline said, breaking the uncomfortable silence at the table.

"Marines, ma'am. I deploy in a few days," he answered in a deep, bass tone.

"And did I hear you say that you were in the Army, Margot?" Caroline prodded.

"That's right. I've been home for about a year now," Margot answered after a mouthful of soup.

"Well, thank you both so much for your service," Caroline said with a bright smile.

"Nana, they hate when people say that. It's like hypocritical," Valerie said loudly.

Margot said nothing to Valerie's comment but smiled to herself. She knew some soldiers who felt that way. However, if her host wanted to thank her for what she'd done for her country, she'd accept the statement of gratitude. Dennis stayed silent, too. His face turned stony as he focused on the food in front of him.

Out of the corner of her eye, Margot noticed Kalina lean in and whisper something to her husband. He waved her off and she let out an audible huff of annoyance. The woman beside Dennis remained quiet throughout the whole meal.

"I don't think caught your name," Margot said, hoping to pull the young woman into the conversation.

Her gaze flickered toward Margot. "Cecelia," she mumbled.

"What brings you to Collingwood?" Margot asked.

"Just visiting," Cecelia mumbled into her napkin.

The conversation died down again as everyone focused on finishing their meals. Maybe it was her pastoral training, but Margot sensed Cecelia needed someone to lean on and open up to. Unfortunately, as soon as she finished eating, Cecelia had quickly retreated upstairs.

"Why don't I show you to your room so you can get settled?" Caroline said, appearing at Margot's side.

"Sure. Thank you."

Margot retrieved her bag. She waited while Caroline checked her in on a slender tablet and then followed the woman up to the second floor.

"Now, we've got a half bath on this floor. Though if you need a shower, you'll have to go up to the third floor," Caroline explained.

Margot nodded mutely as she stepped into a quaint little bedroom with a queen-sized bed and accent pillows. It looked quite inviting with what she guessed was a hand-made quilt laid squarely on top of it.

"Does everyone eat meals together?" Margot turned to face Caroline, who stood in the doorway.

"At least breakfast and lunch. Food is usually ready in the morning by about seven."

"Great. Sorry again for arriving so late," Margot repeated.

"Don't you worry about it, dear. Honestly,

it was nice to break up the tension a bit." Caroline took a step into Margot's room and glanced out into the hallway.

Margot recognized the gesture for what it was. Her host was about to share whatever gossip she had on the other guests ... whether Margot wanted to hear it or not.

"Now, normally I don't like to talk about people," Caroline said, "but this is not how I expected to spend my holiday. Kalina and Chris, the married couple across the hall from you, have spent the entire time bickering. And poor Cecelia ... well she jumps at her own shadow."

"Is she here alone?" Margot bit her tongue the moment the words were out of her mouth.

"No. She arrived with Dennis, but they're in two separate rooms up on the third floor. I can't put my finger on it, but there's something off about the pair of them."

"I'm sure it's nothing," Margot said. Still,

she couldn't help wondering if perhaps Cecelia needed a kind shoulder to lean on. A stranger who wouldn't judge her.

"If you don't mind, I'm going to just take a quick peek upstairs and get the lay of the land," Margot fibbed.

"Of course."

Caroline retreated to the first floor and Margot ascended to the top level of the house. She spotted three doors on the hall. The first revealed the bathroom. The second was empty with a military bag sitting neatly at the foot of the bed. That left the room with its door mostly closed. She approached, knocked twice, and waited.

"Go away," Cecelia called through the doorway.

"Is everything okay? You seem upset," Margot replied.

"I'm fine. Please just leave me alone."

Margot wanted to push, but she knew better. Whatever was weighing on the girl wouldn't be lifted, especially if Margot tried to force the issue.

"Well, if you need someone to talk to, I'm just downstairs one level." Margot returned to her own room, offering up a tiny prayer that everything would look brighter in the morning. After all, it would be a brand-new year. As Margot settled in across from the window, she could see distant flashes of color as the locals let off some early fireworks displays to celebrate the occasion.

MARGOT WASN'T sure what woke her at first. She sat up, wide awake in the unfamiliar room, and looked around. Something had roused her, but what? She checked her phone and saw it was 6:10 in the morning.

Climbing out of bed, she pulled on the jeans and sweater she'd worn the day before and crept into the hallway. The door across the hall remained closed and she moved with quiet steps to the landing leading both up to the top floor and down to the first floor.

Her gut told her to head downstairs, and she did her best to move quietly on the worn wood. It creaked and betrayed her presence as she reached the bottom. She passed the dining room, the table empty but ready for the next meal, and entered the kitchen. A pot of coffee sat on the percolator and by the tiny drops marring the countertop, someone had already taken some. She poured herself a cup after rummaging through two cupboards to find a mug.

Standing with the mug in hand, she gazed out the window above the sink. She caught a glimpse of messy blond hair disappearing out of view. Then the back door opened, and Cecelia entered, looking dazed. Her shoes were caked in snow and she wore no coat, only a bulky sweatshirt with her hands pulled inside the sleeves. Her entire frame shook from the frigid temperature.

"What were you doing outside without a coat?" Margot prompted, guiding the girl to stand away from the partially open door.

"I'm fine," Cecelia answered, teeth chattering together.

"You're not fine. You're freezing. Wait here, I'll find a blanket," Margot said, using her Army-trained authoritative tone.

Cecelia flinched, but stayed put while Margot went in search of a blanket. She pulled open every door on the first floor until she found a linen closet with some shawls. She grabbed two and returned to the kitchen, where she draped them over Cecelia's shoulders.

"Do you drink coffee?" Margot asked. "I can make you some."

Cecelia shook her head. "No. I'm just going to go take a hot shower."

Margot eyed the girl as she pulled the

shawls tighter around her torso and traipsed up the stairs. Margot grabbed a third shawl from the closet and stepped onto the front porch. The early morning air was crisp, but not nearly as cold as she had expected. The night had been windy, blowing snow drifts into new formations. It wasn't enough to obscure the dark smudge of fabric on the ground at the base of the front porch. She set her mug of coffee down on the railing and descended to the front walk.

Dread filled the pit of her stomach. *Please Lord, don't let this be another test of strength.* After uncovering the truth to Port Marie's pain-filled past, she wasn't sure she was willing or even able to take on the pain of another town.

Still, she bent down in the snow and felt the slope of what could be a shoulder. Her mouth went dry and her fingers trembled in the cold morning air. Did she really want to know what lay beneath the snow?

The slushy, biting feeling of snow on her bare hands sent shivers down Margot's spine as she continued to clear it away. She didn't pay attention to the change in skin color as her hands dug deeper into the pile, her gaze zeroing in on the fabric of a shirt and bare arm.

She bit back a cry of surprise, her mind already working to fill her head with gruesome images of what she was inches away from discovering. Despite knowing better, she kept digging until she uncovered the frostbitten and very dead body of Dennis Parker.

As Margot gazed down at the partially uncovered body, she wondered how long he'd been out there. Going against her better judgment, she continued to dig Dennis free, revealing a bullet wound in his chest. *My God.* Was a gunshot the thing that had roused her from sleep?

The sound of the front door slamming against the front of the house drew Margot's attention from the soldier's lifeless body. Kalina appeared on the porch wrapped in a heavy coat, her red curls a mess in the early morning light.

"What's going on?" She asked.

"It's Dennis. He's been shot," Margot answered.

"What? Are you sure?" Kalina was off the porch and by Margot's side in seconds. She crouched down to study the young man's prone form, her hands covering her mouth in shock. "This can't be happening."

"I know this must be unsettling, but we need to call the police," Margot said.

Kalina shook her head and stood up. "Not really. I've seen more dead bodies than you'd think. I sort of have a knack for happening upon them. It drives Chris nuts. Well at least it used to, anyway. Once I'm in it, I can't let go until I know what's happened."

Had Margot found a kindred spirit?

"I'm the same way," Margot murmured. After a beat, she nudged the other woman's shoulder. "We need to call the police and report this."

"My phone is back in my room. I'll get it and tell Chris what's happened."

"I'll stay with Dennis," Margot said and stood at attention. She waited until Kalina was inside before she saluted the dead soldier. "I'm so sorry. I hope you rest in peace," she whispered.

She glanced down at her ungloved hands, realizing that in her effort to uncover Dennis, she'd gotten some of his blood on her. She shivered and fought the urge to wipe them clean. It felt like an eternity before Kalina finally reappeared, Chris trailing her in a t-shirt and unbuttoned jacket. He had a phone pressed to his ear. "This is Captain Christian Harper, Ellesworth Police. I'm at Belvedere B&B, we need police and the coroner. One of the guests is dead."

Kalina slipped past her husband and rejoined Margot by the body. Chris ended the call and closed the distance so all three of them stood over Dennis' partially uncovered body.

"Police are on the way," Chris said. Looking at Margot, he added, "Mind telling me what you were doing out here?"

"You don't have to answer that. He's not in charge," Kalina quipped.

"It's okay," Margot said. "I woke up. I wasn't really sure what roused me at first, although now I think it might have been a gunshot. I came downstairs, stepped outside, and noticed some fabric in the snow. I uncovered him enough to determine his identity. Kalina went inside and got you so we could alert the proper authorities."

"Don't give me that look," Kalina said to her husband.

"I didn't say a word, Kal. Just … stay out of the way, okay?" He rubbed his arms and turned to the front of the house. "I'm going back inside to let Mrs. Belvedere know what's going on, so she doesn't have a heart attack when uniforms show up."

"I don't mean to pry, but is everything okay between you two?" Margot asked Kalina once Chris was out of earshot. The tension she'd observed at dinner the night before still remained.

"We're fine," the other woman answered with a sigh. "We just needed to get away from home for a few days. My sister and nephew are watching the shop I own, and our daughter is with them. We haven't really had a lot of time with just the two of us since she was born. I think he's just frustrated that we can't even go on vacation without death finding us."

"Understandable." Margot replied, her ears perking up at the sound of wailing sirens in the distance growing closer. "You didn't hear the sound of gunshots? It didn't wake you?"

Kalina shook her head. "I'm a pretty

heavy sleeper." She turned away from Dennis' body and asked, "Do you think he's been out here long?"

"I'm no expert. The cold weather probably won't make it easy to determine things for the police, either. Still if what I heard was right, he couldn't have been out here for not much more than an hour or two," Margot noted. "I can't imagine who would want to hurt him."

"I heard him and Cecelia arguing last night after dinner," Kalina said in a hushed tone.

"I tried to talk to her, but she told me to leave. So, I did," Margot said. After a pause, she added, "She was acting strange this morning. She'd been outside in the backyard with no coat or anything. She was nearly frozen when she came back inside."

"You left that part out of what you told Chris."

Margot brushed strands of hair out of her

face. "Honestly, I didn't think it was relevant. But now that you mention her arguing with Dennis … do you know what sort of relationship they had?"

"I mean, they showed up together, but I think they were staying in separate rooms."

Margot was about to mention the fading bruises she'd spotted on the girl's wrists, but decided to keep quiet. She didn't want to accuse Dennis of something he might not have done or agitate Cecelia as it was most certainly a touchy subject.

"Sounds like we should have a chat with her," Kalina said.

3

Margot didn't want to admit the mystery intrigued her. She didn't have time to respond to Kalina before Caroline came barreling out the front door in a bathrobe and slippers. The sirens keened louder, and a squad car, bearing the words Collingwood Police on the side, arrived. Kalina's husband, Chris, marched out behind Caroline and the group of four met the uniformed officer.

"I'm Officer Kevin Johns. Which one of you called about a dead body?"

"I did. He's over here," Chris said.

Caroline followed Chris' movements with her gaze, keeping a safe distance. The moment she laid eyes on Dennis, she let out a high-pitched scream and staggered backward. Margot and Kalina moved in unison to catch her before she fell into the snow. Some of the blood from Margot's hands smeared on the back of Caroline's bathrobe.

"He's really dead?" Caroline whimpered.

"I'm afraid so. Come on, let's get you back inside. I'm sure Officer Johns can talk to us in there," Kalina said softly.

Margot glanced over her shoulder as the other officer accompanying Officer Johns positioned himself by the body, unrolling police tape and tying it to a nearby phone pole. His dark complexion stood out in stark contrast to the wintry scene around him. She and Kalina settled Caroline at the dining room table.

"Fifteen years of owning this place and I've never had a boarder die," Caroline moaned.

"It's going to be okay," Margot assured her, despite not knowing if things would work out. Though she had faith.

"What's going on? Uh … Why are there cops here?" Valerie asked, appearing at the bottom of the stairs in an extra-large t-shirt and pajama pants.

"Mr. Parker is dead," her grandmother replied.

"What? No way." Valerie peered out the front door. "What happened?"

"We aren't sure," Margot replied before too much misinformation could spread around the tiny house.

Valerie backed away from the door as heavy footsteps clomped up the porch. Chris led Officer Johns into the dining room.

"Is this everyone?" Officer Johns asked.

"No, there's one other boarder. I saw her before I went outside. She was taking a shower," Margot answered.

"Where's the bathroom?" He asked.

"She's a young girl. I'm not sure it's appropriate for you to go traipsing into the bathroom when she's indisposed," Kalina said, standing up. "I'll let her know you're here and want to talk to her."

The officer looked irritated, but he nodded and turned to Margot. "I'm told you found the body?"

"Yes, sir."

"I'll need to take your statement and process you for evidence." He gestured to everyone else in the room. "The rest of you stay put. I'll need to talk to you, too."

Margot followed him to the kitchen where he took out a small pad and pen.

"What's your name and what are you doing here?" He asked.

"Reverend Margot Quade. I'm here to celebrate New Year's Eve, although I'm not sure how that's relevant."

"Not spending it with family?" He probed, setting Margot on edge.

"I needed a little peace to myself. You can check with the proprietor. I have a reservation."

He nodded and cleared his throat. "Tell me what happened."

"I went out to the front porch about half an hour ago with a cup of coffee and I spotted something dark against the snow drift. I investigated and found Private Parker," Margot answered.

"How well did you know the deceased?"

"I didn't. Dennis Parker and I met briefly last night at dinner. From what he said, he was in the Marines and would be deploying in a few days. That was the extent of our conversation."

The other officer, whose name plate upon closer inspection identified him as Officer Vargas, appeared in the kitchen to hand over an evidence bag and wallet with a loose ID. Officer Johns glanced at the ID. "To confirm, this is *Devon* Parker."

Margot's brow furrowed. "No, Sir. His name is Dennis."

Officer Johns flashed the ID for Margot to see. It bore a photo that looked like the man she'd met the night before. Only the name on the ID was indeed Devon, not Dennis. "I'm confident he said his name was Dennis."

He gestured to her hands. "Never been to a crime scene, I take it?"

She didn't appreciate his tone, as if she was uneducated. "He could have still been alive. I realize I dislodged snow from the wound that transferred to me. I have done my best not to touch anything until you can process me. However, I can assure you, I did not disturb any other evidence."

Officer Johns tossed the evidence bag on the counter beside him. "Did you notice anything suspicious or out of the ordinary?"

"Other than a dead body?" Margot pressed, hoping he wouldn't ask her more questions about Cecelia.

"Other than that. What do you know about the other guests?" He answered with an accompanying eye roll.

"Not much. I only met them all last night and had very little interaction with them."

"This other boarder who is conveniently indisposed, what do you know about her?"

"Nothing," she answered through pursed lips. Kalina was right, though. Someone needed to talk to Cecelia and see what she really knew about the dead man out front.

"That's all for now. Don't leave the premises. I may have more questions. Someone will process you shortly."

Margot nodded and watched Officer Johns make his way toward the front hall. "Officer?" She called.

He pivoted on his heel. "What?"

"He was about to deploy. Someone ought to notify the military that he won't be showing up for duty."

"You seem awfully interested in his life."

"Just looking out for a fellow soldier." The cross and dog tags hung in plain view around her neck.

"Let us handle things, miss."

Margot bristled at the way he addressed her before he marched back outside. Officer Vargas produced another evidence bag and scraped some of the blood and snow from her fingers.

"Is he always so friendly?" Margot asked.

Officer Vargas shook his head. "He thinks he's a hot shot detective. I'd just do what he asks, and everything will be fine." He pointed to her clothing. "If you'll change out of these clothes, you'll be all set, Reverend. You can wash your hands now, too."

"Thank you."

After scrubbing her palms until they were raw, Margot retreated to her room on the second floor and discarded her clothing, stowing them in the bag the officer had given her. She pulled on a clean sweater and saw a missed call from Sam. She hit redial and pressed the phone to her ear.

"Hey, how's the bed and breakfast?" Sam quipped when she answered.

"Not nearly as restful as I'd hoped. One of the guests is dead. It looks like he was shot," Margot answered, pacing the distance from the door to the exterior wall and back again.

"You're kidding."

Margot shook her head even though Sam couldn't see her. "Afraid not. Sam, there is something off about everything."

The door to her room swung inward and Kalina appeared, her face flushed.

"I'll fill you in when I know more," Margot answered and ended the call. To Kalina, she said, "What's wrong?"

Kalina's face was pale. "Cecelia's gone."

4

"What do you mean *gone?* She said she was going to take a shower to warm up."

Kalina motioned for Margot to follow her. They arrived at the bathroom to find the shower on full blast, steam fogging the mirror above the sink. There was no sign anyone had gotten into the shower stall.

"Where is she?" Margot asked.

"Let's check her room," Kalina said and shut off the water.

The door was closed, and Margot got no

answer when she knocked. She didn't like barging in on someone, but she turned the handle and the door swung inward. The room was not unlike the one Margot had been given, with a bed against one wall and a dresser on the opposite one. There were no bags in sight.

"Did she leave?" Margot wondered aloud.

"We would have seen her," Kalina muttered.

Not if she went out the back. Margot stepped out of the room and closed the door. None of this made sense. "Are you sure she and Dennis knew each other?"

Kalina nodded, auburn curls bouncing against her cheeks. "They showed up around the same time Chris and I did. They were in one car, but both were very particular about having different rooms."

"This is all so strange. The officer who questioned me said the identification they found with Dennis said his name was Devon."

"That can't be right. I heard Cecelia call him Dennis."

Margot shrugged. "I saw the ID. It had a different name, but it definitely was his picture. We need to find Cecelia. If she knows something, she needs to tell the police. Besides even if she's in the dark, she needs to know her friend is dead."

Before Kalina could say anything more, Margot retreated to the second floor to retrieve her clothing for the police. She found Officer Johns in a heated discussion with Chris.

"You aren't going to just come in here accusing my wife of something without any tangible evidence," Chris argued.

"I didn't say anything about accusing her. I need to talk to her to see what she knows about this missing guest."

"Who's missing?" Margot interrupted.

Chris let out an exasperated sigh. "Cecelia."

"Her room is empty. No bags or anything," Kalina said.

"And how do you know that?" Officer Johns demanded.

"Because I looked when I went up to let her know you wanted to speak with her. I'm happy to give a statement about what I know," Kalina said, stepping up so she was even with Margot. As the officer and Chris exchanged mutual looks of distrust, Kalina whispered in Margot's ear, "Figure out where Cecelia went. I'll keep him busy."

5

After handing off the evidence bag of clothing to Officer Vargas, Margot retreated to her room to give Sam another call. Her cousin answered on the first ring. "What's going on?"

"Like I said before, a guest was found shot to death this morning. There seems to be a mix-up with his identification. Can you run the name Dennis Parker and see if anything comes up? I've got a bad feeling about all of this and can't seem to shake it."

"I'll see what I can find. But if he's never

set foot in Port Marie, I doubt I'll find any-thing useful."

"Thanks for checking anyway," Margot said. "One of the other guests is missing. She might have information about who wanted to hurt the victim."

"I thought you went on this little getaway to … you know … get away from all of this getting mixed up with murders stuff."

Kalina had said much the same thing and Margot let out a small laugh. "I did. And I'm not the only one, apparently. I'm going to do some more digging and see what I can find out. Call me if you find anything."

She ended the call and stowed her phone in her pocket. Knowing she was about to do some not-entirely-legal snooping, she donned her winter gloves before making the trek to the third floor again. With only two officers on scene, they likely hadn't had time to process Cecelia's or Dennis' rooms. She reentered Cecelia's first. The lack of belongings still set Margot on edge. The girl must have come with clothes and other items one typically brings when staying away from home. *Unless she hadn't had time to bring much with her?*

Margot checked under the bed—which had clearly not been slept in the night before—and moved to the closet. With one hand on the knob, she paused, listening to the space around her. Her military training told her something was off here, but she couldn't quite put her finger on it. She eased the closet door open and found a duffle bag with a few sweaters and a pair of jeans stuffed haphazardly inside.

If Cecelia was still around, she'd left her things behind. Although Margot still couldn't wrap her head around what would give the young woman a motive to kill Private Parker.

Perhaps Margot would have better luck in his room.

She heard the heavy fall of footsteps on the stairs below her just as she reached the second room in the hallway. A crash from within the room drew her attention and she nudged the door open with her foot.

Cecelia leaned over an unmade bed, sheets and blankets bunched to the foot. Fatigues lay sprawled on the floor, the rest of Dennis's belongings strewn about. Cecelia looked up as the door swung inward with a soft *hiss*.

"What are you doing in here?" She demanded.

"I was going to ask you the same thing. I thought you came up here to take a shower," Margot replied.

Cecelia at least appeared to have changed into dry clothes.

"It's none of your business," Cecilia muttered.

Margot stepped forward, holding her hands loosely at her side in a non-threatening manner. "You may think it isn't, but there are police downstairs. A man is dead. And I have to admit, you rifling through someone else's belongings isn't going to make you look innocent." She couldn't bring herself to say the word 'guilty,' because she couldn't fathom why this young girl would shoot anyone.

"Who's dead?" Cecelia rasped.

"It looks like Private Parker," Margot answered, moving to sit by the other woman. While she didn't see a reason for Cecelia to be the culprit, she also wasn't going to share any information she'd gained from the police with her either.

"Cecelia, can you tell me how you know Private Parker?"

"I don't know him," she said quickly, her hands twisting into knots in her lap.

"That's not what I've heard from other people. They said you came together."

"They're wrong. We just arrived at the

same time." Cecelia stood up and moved to the doorway. "I don't know him, but he can't be dead."

"Want to explain why you were going through a stranger's belongings, then?"

"I thought he took something of mine. I was wrong." She wiped at her eyes, revealing ashen bruises on her left wrist. She saw Margot looking and quickly tugged the hem down. "Can I go back to my room now?'

"I think it might be better if you went downstairs to talk to the police. Give your statement before you do anything else."

"Oh, yeah I guess I can do that." Cecelia cast one last look around the room before Margot led her back to the first floor.

Shouts from the front hall erupted as they reached the landing. Officer Johns shoved Kalina toward a wall, pulling out a pair of handcuffs.

"Get your hands off my wife," Chris bellowed, trying to get between the officer and Kalina.

"We found the weapon in your wife's bag," Officer Johns said with a far-too-casual shrug. He gestured with his free hand to a handgun sitting in a clear evidence bag on the reception desk.

"I don't own a gun," Kalina's voice was strained and the color drained from her cheeks, making her red curls stand out even more against her pale face.

"Sir, shouldn't we test her hands for gunshot residue before we jump to such conclusions?" Officer Vargas suggested.

Officer Johns glared at the man, then caught sight of Margot and Cecelia in the small space.

Margot cleared her throat. "This is Cecelia. She's ready to give her statement."

Cecelia's eyes turned the size of saucers at the sight of Officer Johns. The other officer stepped up and put a hand on the girl's shoulder. She flinched at his touch and he took a step back.

"I'll take your statement if you wouldn't mind coming with me," Officer Vargas said softly, leading Cecelia away from the scene in the front hall.

Margot stepped up beside Chris. "I'm sure we can sort this all out. Kalina came outside with me shortly after I discovered the body."

"Besides, I have no reason to kill anyone. I didn't know him," Kalina insisted, struggling against the officer's grip. "Please, test my hands. You'll see I haven't fired a gun."

Officer Johns' gaze shifted from Margot, to Chris, to Kalina, and back. With an unnecessarily rough shove, he released his grasp and disappeared out to his patrol car.

"What is his problem?" Kalina hissed before he returned.

"He probably wants to prove himself, so he's trying to solve this case fast rather than doing his due diligence. I'm tempted to report him to his superiors," Chris grumbled.

Officer Johns returned and swabbed Kalina's hands, a scowl tugging at his pale cheeks. "Fine." He turned to Margot and Chris. "Any objection if I test you two as well?"

Chris held his hands out. "Go ahead."

Officer Johns swabbed his and then Margot's hands. A look of disappointment fell over his face as he came up negative on all three of them. He stormed out of the house again, this time climbing into the passenger seat of the patrol car and slamming the door. Margot had expected him to test everyone in the house. Surely it would have given a quick answer as to whether anyone had fired a gun.

"Is he going to test everyone else?" She turned to Officer Vargas.

"I'm sure he will," he answered and

turned to Cecelia, ushering her into the kitchen to take her statement.

"What was that all about?" Caroline appeared from the dining room. She seemed more composed than when the police had first arrived.

"Just a misunderstanding," Kalina said and rubbed at her forearm.

"Did they find Cecelia?" Caroline's tone carried a hint of accusation, as if she'd already decided the girl had a hand in why there was a dead man on her front lawn.

"She's giving her statement," Margot answered.

There were still too many missing pieces to this puzzle and Margot couldn't help wanting to find out what they were. She'd barely known Private Parker, but she felt a kinship to another man in uniform. He deserved to see justice done.

"Can I talk to you?" She whispered, nudging Kalina's shoulder.

The two women retreated to the second-floor landing.

When she felt they had privacy, Margot whispered, "I found Cecelia going through Private Parker's room. She said she thought he'd taken something of hers. Also, I noticed a few old bruises on her wrists. Like someone had grabbed her and pulled hard."

Kalina nodded. "I noticed them, too. You don't think Dennis … or Devon or whatever his name is hurt her?"

Margot shrugged. "Someone clearly did. She denied knowing him when I talked to her just now. Although I could tell she was lying."

"Chris would say I'm a little too nosy, but I watched the two of them interact. If anything, it looked like he was helping her."

"I reached out to my cousin who is an officer in the police department back home, just to see if anything comes up in the criminal database."

"Chris did the same, but hasn't heard back yet."

"As much as I don't want to believe Cecelia could have pulled the trigger, she was acting strange this morning. I caught her sneaking inside from the back of the house and she wasn't in a coat. It was like she'd gone outside in a hurry and was trying to hide something." Margot stepped into the bedroom she'd been assigned and peered out the window. "Whoever killed Dennis tried to frame you. Any idea why they'd pick you?"

Kalina joined her by the window and shook her head. "Honestly, no. I mean, we don't know for sure that the gun they found is the murder weapon."

"Officer Johns seemed to think so. There's something off about him."

"I think Chris is right and he's just trying to prove himself," Kalina replied.

Margot had her doubts. From the moment he'd arrived at the tiny bed and breakfast, Officer Johns had been hurrying through his investigation and then ignoring easy ways to rule out suspects. She longed to have Sam working the case. At least then Margot knew the police wouldn't do a rush job just to get closure.

As she gazed down at the snowbanks filling the back yard, she spotted footprints along the back of the house. The wind had been whipping around as the morning progressed. If the footprints had been old, the weather would have obscured them. These were fresh.

"I want to know what Cecelia was looking for upstairs," Kalina announced, interrupting Margot's focus.

Kalina was out of the room and on the flight of stairs leading to the top floor before Margot had time to process her words. Should she follow the other woman or investigate the footprints? She pulled out her phone and zoomed in as much as she could before snapping a few photos of the tracks from her vantage point.

By the time she reached Private Parker's room, Kalina was standing in the doorway, mouth agape. Margot squeezed past the other woman to find the room was empty. The fatigues and pack were gone. It looked as if Private Parker had packed up and shipped out without anyone noticing.

"This just keeps getting stranger," Margot murmured just as her phone rang. She pressed it to her ear without checking the caller ID. "Hello?"

"Margot, it's Sam. I didn't find anything on a Dennis Parker in our records other than he was issued a driver's license when he was sixteen. But I've got quite a few open warrants for a Devon Parker, same date of birth."

"Thanks, Sam."

Who is this man?

6

The two women stood side by side in the room silently as the situation settled over them. Kalina was the first to recover from the shock.

"There's got to be an explanation for all of this. Why would he have a driver's license in the same state with two different names?" She asked.

Margot was beginning to suspect one possibility—brothers, perhaps. "What if it's two different people?"

"What, you think he's got a criminal twin brother out there?" Kalina scoffed.

Margot nodded. "Why not? It would explain why the man we met had a different name. I bet if we were to check military records, we would find that Private Dennis Parker is set to deploy in a couple days just like he said."

"But how did Devon end up dead, then? And if that is in fact Devon out there, where'd Dennis go?"

All good questions to which Margot didn't have any answers. There was more to the story with Cecelia, and they needed to find out what it was.

"I have an idea, but it's not exactly legal," Margot said, lowering her voice out of an abundance of caution.

"I'm listening." Kalina's green eyes sparkled with anticipation.

"We both get the sense there's more to the connection between Dennis and Cecelia.

Officer Johns doesn't seem in a hurry to process her room or Dennis' either. We could take another look around. Just to see if we missed something."

Kalina smiled, but arched a brow. "You have this look like you're about to crawl out of your skin. The idea of doing something questionably legal makes you uncomfortable, doesn't it?"

"Of course, it does. I spent years in a military command structure. Disobeying one's superiors or stepping out of line wasn't just frowned upon. It was met with swift repercussions. Besides, as a reverend, I'm not exactly happy about breaking the law."

"Well, like you said, it isn't really a crime scene, yet."

The conversation died when footsteps signaled that they had company in the hallway. A light knock on the door preceded Chris' appearance. He said, "The officers have left for now, but they asked that everyone stay put for additional questioning as needed."

"They think the real crime happened outside, too. And they've got the murder weapon. It should be easy to figure out who had it last," Kalina said.

He cleared his throat and nudged the door shut behind him. "If I were running this investigation, I'd have moved everyone off premises and closed this whole place off as a crime scene, no matter if the crime occurred outside. I can't believe these guys are that incompetent. I've put in a call to some friends to see what I can find on Officer Johns and his partner."

"We think Dennis may have had a brother," Margot shared. If she was comfortable enough to share the theory with Kalina, she figured it was safe to voice it with Kalina's husband. After all, had Sam been there, Margot would've done the same thing. "We can do some low-key digging. Nothing that would run afoul of the law, just to confirm. If we can give the officers any other information, I'm sure they wouldn't say no."

Kalina looped her arm through Chris' and gazed at him. "That's how we work."

The forced smile on Chris' face told Margot he wasn't thrilled about his wife's statement, although he didn't contradict it. Chris detached himself from his wife's embrace and gave them both a pointed look. "I'm going to check on our host. I'll let her know you two will be down in twenty minutes for an early lunch."

He left them in Margot's room in silence.

Margot couldn't hide her surprise. "Did he really just gave us a window to look around?"

"He doesn't always like it when I nose in on a case, but he's accepted by this point that it's bound to happen. I know we came here to get away from the drama, but I guess we just aren't that lucky."

Or maybe it had nothing to do with luck. Margot had come here seeking the same sort of refuge, but clearly God had other plans. She couldn't believe it was a coincidence that she and Kalina were here at the same time.

"Come on," Margot said. "Let's see what we can find in Cecelia's room before we have to see Caroline about lunch."

They trekked up to the third floor again and entered the first room past the bathroom. The closet with Cecelia's meager belongings remained open. Margot had remembered to bring along her gloves again and pulled the bag loose from its hiding place. She set the contents on the bed. As she'd observed earlier, there were only a couple changes of clothes along with a cell phone buried at the very bottom of the bag. Margot picked it up and had her finger poised to hit the Power button when a sharp intake of breath from behind her stopped Margot mid-motion. Both she and Kalina turned to see Cecelia standing in the door-way, white as a sheet.

"We know you're scared by everything that's going on right now, but we want to help," Margot said, setting the phone on the bed in what she hoped was a gesture of goodwill. She was giving Cecelia a chance to reveal whatever secrets might be hidden on the phone.

"Please, talk to us. We can help, we promise," Kalina added. "How did you know Dennis?"

Cecelia tugged on the sleeves of her over-sized sweater. "He's my friend. He was helping me get out of a bad situation. Or at least I thought he was. Now he's missing."

"Did his brother Devon have anything to do with the 'bad situation' you were in?" Margot asked.

Cecelia burst into tears.

"Come on," Margot said, patting the bed. "Sit down and tell us what happened."

7

ecelia slumped onto the bed, drawing her knees to her chest. She looked so young staring up at them behind long lashes with dark eyes. Margot suspected she was trying to hide within herself out of a sense of fear.

"Things were great at first. Devon was funny and charming. But, after a while things got … complicated." Cecelia tugged at her sleeves again.

"He hurt you," Margot said softly, and she nodded.

"He'd always apologize after. He would just get upset sometimes. I knew it wasn't right, but most of the time he was so sweet. I felt like maybe a part of me was just overreacting. Then Dennis came over one time and he saw Devon get upset. The two of them got into a fight. I thought Dennis was going to kill Devon. He beat him up pretty badly. Threatened to do worse if he laid a hand on me again."

Cecelia's shoulders relaxed as the words poured out of her. Margot was beginning to get an idea of where this story was leading, and it wasn't good. "How long ago was that?"

The young woman kneaded her hands together, her gaze darting between Margot and Kalina. "A few weeks ago. Honestly, I was more surprised that Devon had a twin brother. The more I thought about it, I realized it was kind of weird that he never talked about his family. Well that and he didn't want me to meet them."

"But you met Dennis and he defended you," Kalina reiterated.

Cecelia nodded. "Things got really bad a couple days ago and Devon lost his temper." She pushed up the sleeves of her sweater to reveal the bruises Margot had caught sight of earlier. "He grabbed me so hard I thought he was going to break my wrists. I called Dennis and he told me to pack a bag and go to the bus stop near where I work. He met me there and we came here."

"You were very brave to make the choice to get away from Devon," Margot said.

"Dennis said he would help me get out of town without Devon knowing before he deployed. We were supposed to leave tomorrow."

"Did you ever go to the police for help?" Kalina blurted.

Margot turned toward the other woman, wanting to admonish her, but finding Kalina's cheeks were already flushed in embarrassment. Gently, Margot said, "She sought help where she could."

"I called the police a couple times at first, but nothing happened," Cecelia said. "They would show up, Devon would tell them everything was fine, and they would leave."

Margot had to imagine the police force was small in town. Sam had mentioned Devon had a criminal record. Sam hadn't elaborated, but perhaps another call was in order. Or perhaps Chris would find something useful from his own search.

"Do you think Dennis was actually capable of harming his brother?" Margot clasped her hands in her lap. She wanted to physically comfort the woman in front of her, but she didn't know if physical contact would trigger negative feelings in Cecelia. She wanted to help, not hurt.

"I had to pull him off the last time. It was really hard so, yeah … I think he could."

Margot glanced at her phone to check the

time. Their window for snooping was about to expire. Chris expected them both downstairs to share a meal with their hostess. "Thank you for sharing. I think Caroline is putting together some food downstairs for lunch. Why don't you join us?"

Cecelia fidgeted, but swung her legs over the side of the bed and stood up. "You aren't going to tell anyone what I told you, are you?"

Before Margot could say she couldn't make promises, Kalina mimed zipping her lips and tossing away the key. "Come on, let's go get something to eat."

Margot watched the two women disappear down the hallway. Something about Cecelia's story bothered Margot. She showed signs of discomfort when sharing her history with her abusive boyfriend. Still Margot had expected more emotion, given that all signs pointed to the fact he was dead. *Shouldn't she be relieved he's dead?* It was a terrible thought, but it was the one that popped into Margot's head. Cecelia was free of the man who had caused her pain, and yet she still carried him with her like an albatross.

As she stepped into the hallway, the sound of a door creaking on its hinges caught her attention. She paused and held her breath, waiting for the sound to come again, but it didn't. Still, the training she'd relied on for so long overseas told her she wasn't alone. No one had seen Dennis since the night before. If he had lashed out at his brother for some reason, maybe he'd come back to fulfill his promise to Cecelia? Margot moved down the hall to the missing man's room. The door was ajar, and she once again pushed it open. Unlike the last time she'd taken stock of it, it was now empty. Someone had cleared out the space. But who? And why?

Margot was the last one to enter the dining room. She was surprised to see how normal it looked, given the chaos of the morning. She settled in a seat by the front window. Everyone else had crowded as far from the outside view as possible. She glanced out to see a single strip of police tape waving in the winter air. She could spot the disturbed snow where she'd found Devon's body.

"I can't believe someone actually died here," Valerie said, for once not consumed by her phone. "Nana, you have to advertise as the haunted bed and breakfast now. You'll do awesome business at Halloween."

"A man is dead, Valerie. Have some respect," Caroline snapped. Her cheery demeanor from the night before had vanished, replaced by something cold and haunted.

"Just saying," Valerie mumbled into her sandwich.

Margot busied herself with putting together a sandwich of her own, although she didn't feel much like eating. Cecelia sat across the table looking uncomfortable, wedged between Chris and Kalina. Margot gave the young woman a smile and kept the news that it appeared Dennis had taken off to herself. Something about this whole situation seemed strange. If Dennis had indeed shot his brother, why hide the weapon in another guest's belongings? If he was planning to leave, why not take it with him? Certainly, that would ensure it wouldn't be tied back to him.

Although from the little time she'd observed of the man at dinner and what Kalina had shared from his stay before Margot's arrival, running didn't seem like the type of thing Dennis Parker would do. He'd defended a woman he didn't know from his brother's abuse. He'd promised to help her out of a dangerous situation. He didn't seem the type to kill someone and run from the consequences.

"You're awfully quiet, Reverend," Caroline said from Margot's left.

"I'm sorry. I'm still processing everything from this morning. Trying to figure out how it could have happened."

Caroline inclined her head, her gray hair bobbing with the gesture. "I just can't imagine having so much hate in one's heart to take a life."

Margot had witnessed death during her

tour of duty. Some of it a result of the jobs they'd been sent to fulfill. Other times born out of the cruelty of human greed. Knowing a trip down memory lane wasn't beneficial, she said, "I wonder where Dennis has gone, if indeed his brother is dead."

"He did seem like such a nice young man. His poor family, losing one son and the other disappearing."

Margot only nodded in silence. She wanted to take another look in Dennis' room to see if he might have left a clue as to where he'd gone and why he had abandoned Cecelia after promising her safe passage.

"If you don't mind," Margot said, "I think I'm going to head back upstairs. I need a little space."

"Of course," Caroline said, folding her hands on the table.

Margot stood and was halfway out of the dining room when a flash of red curls out of the corner of her eye told her she would not be leaving alone. Margot carried her plate into the kitchen and set it in the sink, Kalina hot on her heels.

"Chris said he hasn't gotten much from Ellesworth PD. Devon had some open warrants and a criminal history mostly related to gambling."

"Cecelia did say he would get angry sometimes. If he was a gambler and was losing, that could trigger outbursts," Margot said softly.

"I wish we could find where Dennis went. If we could just get his side of the story." Kalina sighed.

"I think he's taken off. Before I came down, I heard noise coming from Dennis' room. But when I checked, it was empty."

"Maybe the police took it for evidence?" Kalina's flat tone told Margot that even she didn't believe her own words.

"I don't see how some fatigues and an Army pack would be very useful to the investigation," Margot said, dismissing the suggestion. Still Kalina's words about finding Dennis sparked an idea. "Does Chris have access to Dennis' last known address?"

"He does. What are you thinking?"

"That if we check out where he lives, maybe we can figure out where he's gone."

"Chris wouldn't be happy with me pulling the information," Kalina said, but the glint in her eye told Margot the other woman was willing to risk her husband being unhappy with her if it meant solving the mystery.

"How long do you need to find the information?"

Kalina pursed her lips. "Give me ten minutes. I can meet you out front in fifteen."

MARGOT STOOD on the front porch fifteen minutes later, waiting for Kalina. The spot where they'd taken away Devon's body remained disturbed, although there was far less blood than she would have thought. Maybe the cold had stopped the blood flow prematurely.

"I've got it," Kalina announced as she appeared on the porch and dangled a set of car keys in one hand.

Margot followed the other woman to a small car parked on the street. Kalina plugged the address into her phone's GPS. The system said Dennis' place was only a ten-minute drive away.

"So, how often do you go chasing after potential killers?" Margot asked as Kalina pulled away from the curb.

Kalina laughed. "Not much since we had our daughter. I kind of promised Chris I'd give it up. Besides, it felt like that part of my life was done. I'd put to bed some of my town's old mysteries, you know?"

"I do. In fact, since I've been back home,

I've put to rest several of the painful memories from my own town's past."

"You'd think coming back to a small town would mean less drama. Though I swear there was more death in Ellesworth in a nine-month period than in all of Boston in the entire time I went to school and lived there."

It was Margot's turn to laugh. "I felt the same way after coming home from my deployment. But there's also something nice about helping people to heal. It's partly why I went into ministry. I wanted to use that connection to God to help guide people through dark times. I was able to do it with my unit members overseas, and I like to think I've had a positive impact on the members of my congregation since coming home."

"You just wish you didn't have to do it on vacation." Kalina rolled to a stop at a red light and checked the directions.

"Exactly." Margot agreed.

"You know, while you were giving your statement to the police, I was watching the forensic technician examine Devon's body. I noticed something odd about his hands."

"What do you mean?"

"So, when we were coming downstairs, Cecelia told me that Devon bites his nails. Sort of a nervous habit. But Devon's hands, the nails were neatly trimmed."

"Are you sure? I mean, it's not like you got a good look at his hands."

"I shared enough meals with the man to notice his nails were trimmed."

"So, what are you saying?' Margot prodded.

"I don't know. Maybe Devon let his nails grow out and he started taking better care of them. Or maybe that wasn't actually Devon."

"We both thought it was Dennis at first," Margot said.

"But that's because we didn't know he

had a twin brother. Why would he have his brother's ID on him?"

"I don't know. Let's hope he's at home so we can ask him."

Kalina pulled up to the curb outside a two-story townhouse, the driveway in front of Dennis' unit empty. A silver sedan sat parked in the driveway to the right. Margot thought she caught a flash of movement behind a curtain on the upper level as they climbed out and approached the front door.

Margot knocked twice and rang the bell, hoping it was enough to draw whoever was inside down to the first floor. They waited side by side for a good five minutes before the front door opened and Dennis—or a man who could pass for him—stared out at them. He opened it just wide enough to speak through.

"Hi, we're glad you're at home," Margot said, stepping up and putting her hand on the doorknob.

His five o'clock shadow was more noticeable than the night before and Margot caught the shadow of a bruise forming under his right eye. His gaze didn't register any recognition at the sight of them.

"You look a little confused. It's Margot and Kalina from last night," Margot offered.

"Oh, right. Sorry, I'm kind of busy. What do you want?"

"Well, we were hoping to ask you what you knew about your brother being found dead this morning," Kalina answered.

His eyes narrowed, but he didn't open the door to let them in. "He had what was coming to him."

That didn't sound like the young man she'd met the night before. "What made you take off? You had to know the police needed to take a statement," Margot said.

"I just needed to get out of there, that's all. Too much going on," he said, his gaze darting to the street beyond them.

"Cecelia was worried about you," Margot pressed, trying to inch closer to him.

"Well tell her I'm fine. Look, I need to go. I'll stop by and give the cops a statement."

He slammed the door in their faces. Margot reached out to knock again, but Kalina caught her wrist, stopping her mid-motion. "I don't think knocking again is going to make him any more talkative."

"No, but that also didn't seem to be the same man we met at the bed and breakfast."

"People react differently to stress," Kalina commented. "But, you're right. He didn't have any sort of emotional response when we mentioned his dead brother. Even if they had a contentious relationship, he would have felt *something*."

The front door to the other unit opened and an elderly woman with thick, Coke-bottle glasses stuck her head out. "Something wrong?"

"No, ma'am," Margot answered. Dennis'

neighbors didn't need to be dragged into the mystery of a dead man.

"You know, he told me he was going off to war. Said he wouldn't be coming back for months. Left me his keys and everything. Then he shows up again looking like something's chasing him. I asked him if he was okay, but he just ignored me," she said.

"Deploying is a complicated time," Margot said. She ushered Kalina back to the car as the older woman stepped back into her home. "We need to tell the police what we suspect before he skips town."

9

The trip back to Belvedere B&B took hardly any time at all and what they found upon their return surprised both Margot and Kalina. A small crowd had gathered across the street, ogling the property as if it were a sideshow attraction. Officers Johns and Vargas had returned, the former corralling the onlookers as Margot and Kalina climbed out of the car.

"What's that about?" Kalina wondered aloud as they approached Officer Vargas.

"People in this town are nosy when it

suits them," he answered, glaring at the crowd.

Margot studied the assembled group and noted the mixture of people seemed odd, even for a small town. There were people dressed in suits and ties, messenger bags slung over their chests, and several older women with fur hats who looked like they'd come out of their nearby homes. Also, there was a slender man in a long gray trench coat, standing a little off to one side as Officer Johns addressed them.

"Move along, folks. Nothing to see here."

"Well obviously there is. I'm fairly certain Caroline Belvedere didn't decide to decorate for the new year with police tape," one of the women retorted.

"I'm sure you'll all read about what happened in the paper," Officer Johns replied.

The slender man stepped away from the group, glancing at what Margot guessed was a phone in his hand before walking down the street.

A news van rolled up across the street, drawing Officer Johns' attention. Office Vargas led Margot and Kalina around the back of the house. The footprints Margot had noticed earlier were still visible. He pulled out a pen and pad and nodded for Margot to speak.

"Well, we don't think the man who died is Devon after all," she began. "For one thing, I noticed these boot prints earlier," she continued, gesturing to the footprints in the snow. "I know military boot treads, and all Private Parker had with him were his uniform boots. These were made by a normal boot."

"I see. I'll look into it. Is there anything else that makes you think it wasn't Devon?" Officer Vargas leaned closer, pen poised above his pad.

"Kalina noticed his nails were trimmed,

and we have it on good authority that Devon was a nail biter."

"And how do you know about the nail biting?" He prodded.

"We talked to Cecelia," Margot admitted.

"That would be the same young woman who denied knowing anything about the man you two found?"

Margot hadn't realized Cecelia had been untruthful with the police. Although if she'd had brushes with the law thanks to Devon's abuse and no action had been taken, Margot could see how it might make Cecelia leery of cooperating. Still, lying to the police was a crime, too. "She confided in us that Devon was her boyfriend. She was leaving him, and Private Parker was helping her make a clean break."

Officer Vargas sighed, clipping his pen to his shirt. "I thought she looked familiar. We responded to a few domestic dispute calls, but Officer Johns always handled things."

"What do you mean 'handled things?'" Kalina asked. "From what Cecelia told us, the police would show up, then Devon would convince them everything was fine, and they would leave."

"Honestly, he's my training officer and when he told me to stay in the hallway, I listened. I knew something felt off, but I didn't want to make waves." He gestured to his face. "I don't exactly fit the mold of what a cop looks like in this town. They'd think I was crying wolf to get attention."

"And now a man is dead. Did you run his prints even though you found the ID on him?" Margot pressed.

His caramel complexion paled. "Officer Johns said he ran them and confirmed they belonged to Devon Parker. But … I didn't actually see him run them."

"Is there any reason Officer Johns would want everyone to think Devon is the one who is dead?" Margot thought she might have an idea. At least as to why *Devon* might want people to believe he was dead.

"I can't believe he would. He's a good police officer," he answered.

"Even good police can go bad for the right reasons," Kalina said.

"Look, I'll run the prints again, but whether that's Devon or Dennis, we have our shooter. I don't know what story Cecelia told you, but she's not some innocent victim. We tested her hands and it came back positive for gunshot residue."

Before Kalina or Margot could speak, he retreated around the side of the house.

"You don't think they're right, do you?" Kalina's voice was high with tension.

"It's possible. Anything is. I mean, if she thought she'd killed Devon that would mean she was free from his abuse once and for all. It could explain why she seemed so dispassionate. Maybe she was trying to cover her motives."

"But if it was Dennis she really shot, what motive would she have for that? By her own account, he was basically her savior," Kalina argued.

"They're twins. If it was dark out, if she was afraid, maybe she got confused and shot the wrong brother?" Still that didn't explain how Devon had found them. Margot got the distinct impression Dennis had brought Cecelia here, because Devon didn't know where they were.

"If it turns out that we're right and the man we saw in Dennis' townhouse apartment was in fact Devon, that's going to devastate her."

Commotion from the front of the house drew them back to the front yard. The news van that had pulled up was running cameras on a young-faced male reporter as Officer Johns led Cecelia out the front door in handcuffs.

"There are still pieces of this that don't

fit," Margot murmured. *How did Cecelia get a gun? How had Devon found them? Why was Officer Johns turning a blind eye to the evidence and jumping to conclusions before doing his due diligence?*

"I was thinking the same thing," Kalina said as her husband stepped onto the front porch and gestured for them to join him inside.

They ended up back in the kitchen. "Where are Caroline and her granddaughter?" Margot glanced around for any sign of their hostess.

"In Caroline's room. When the officers came in to arrest Cecelia, things got a little heated. They threatened Caroline with obstruction charges."

"We did some digging, and we think that was really Dennis who was killed," Kalina informed Chris.

"What makes you so sure?"

"We went to Dennis' apartment and the

man there didn't seem to recognize us, and he pretty much told us to leave. Plus, his neighbor said he'd locked up his apartment ahead of his deployment. Left his keys with her in fact, but then he shows up again and in a hurry. I bet you if the police went to his place, they would find it a mess," Kalina explained.

"Besides, if Dennis had been lurking around the place, his boot treads would have shown up in the snow," Margot added. "I spotted treads, but they didn't look like military issue. I thought I'd heard someone in Dennis' room earlier too. It's possible Devon could have snuck in after the police left and collected his brother's belongings to make it appear that Dennis had left."

She expected Chris to admonish them for investigating when they had no right to do so. Sam would certainly have, had she been present. Even if she would have later told Margot she was grateful for the help.

Somehow though, he looked relieved, like he'd had suspicions of his own and they'd just confirmed them.

He said, "I did some asking around—unofficially, of course—and the warrants out for Devon were all related to illegal gambling."

"We found that, too. I suppose if he was in deep with a bookie, maybe faking his death was the best way he could think of to disappear. Impersonate his twin brother who was deploying, and he could go almost anywhere. People wouldn't know to ask the Marine Corp whether he showed up or not. They'd just assume he'd gone overseas," Margot said.

"Great supposition, but how do we prove it?" Kalina leaned against the sink, bumping an empty coffee cup.

"When I came downstairs," Margot said, "there was already a cup of coffee made. I didn't think much of it, but what if Devon had convinced Dennis to see him one last time before he left town and had intended to just share a cup of coffee with his brother before things turned deadly?"

Chris nodded, but he didn't look convinced. "It's all good in theory like Kal said, but we don't have proof."

"Officer Vargas is running the victim's prints again. I wish we could talk to Cecelia, just to get her side of the story. If we knew what she was thinking, maybe we could find a way to help her. If indeed she's the shooter, she's a victim in all of this, as much as whoever she shot," Margot said.

As if on cue, Officer Vargas appeared in the hallway looking grim. He approached their trio, hands in his pockets.

"What's wrong?" Chris asked.

"You two were right. The man you found this morning is Dennis Parker, not Devon. Fingerprints confirm it."

"What does this mean?" Kalina pressed.

Margot and Chris closed in around the officer. They might have been alone in the small space, but whatever he was about to say made it feel like they were about to become conspirators.

"It means my partner lied," he said. "I need to know why."

10

"We want to help in whatever way we can." Margot said after a moment of strained silence. "But, do you think you could get us in to see Cecelia. Just for a few minutes. We have our suspicions as to why she may have done what she did, but we want to be sure. She's a victim, too."

"It's not legal, but I'll see if I can sneak you into holding. I went back over the calls we received and confirmed that she was the caller." Officer Vargas's eyes shone with unshed tears. "All domestic disputes ... and I was there on those calls. I could have done something to help her, but I let my own fear keep me silent. I am not going to do that anymore." After a breath he added, "Come down to the station. I'll do what I can."

"Thank you," Margot replied, squeezing his hand.

After he'd left, she turned to Kalina and Chris. "See what you can find on Officer Johns. He fits into this puzzle somehow. I am starting to think it's more than just looking the other way on domestic disputes. I'm going to talk to Cecelia and see if she'll confirm what we've speculated."

She had one other stop she wanted to make, too.

THE TRIP to the station was a brisk walk, but Margot didn't mind the fresh air or the time to think in private. The crowd had dispersed once Cecelia had been arrested, although Margot suspected the local news would be replaying the scene during the evening news. Too bad they had the wrong story. Or at the very least, not the whole story.

She was within twenty paces of the station when her phone range. Sam's face flashed on the screen.

"Hey, Sam. Now's not the best time to talk," Margot answered.

"Oh, I was just calling to see how you were doing. I know this isn't your first body, but it's the first one you can't look into."

How wrong you are. "An arrest has been made, but I don't think the police have the full picture. I'm trying to see what I can do to help the truth get out."

"So, you aren't staying out of it." Sam's tone was amused rather than annoyed or disapproving.

"You know me, Sam. You couldn't possibly think I wouldn't seek justice. Look, when everything's been sorted out, I'll tell you all about it. I promise."

"You better. And be careful, okay? I want my cousin to come home in one piece."

She ended the call and walked into the tiny station. The officer she was looking for stood out in the smattering of sparsely populated desks. He met her at the entrance to the bull pen and ushered her to the back where two cells took up most of the available space. Cecelia sat in one of the cells, pressed in the corner.

"I can buy you five minutes," the officer said. "Ten at most. So, be quick."

"Thank you again, Officer. I know this is not playing by the rules."

He shook his head. "Be quick," he repeated before leaving the two women alone.

"What are you doing here?" Cecelia asked, her tone hoarse. Redness under her eyes signaled she'd been crying.

"I wanted to hear your side of the story, Cecelia. Please, it might help."

The other woman gave a bitter laugh. "Help? There's nothing you can do."

"Telling someone else what happened might make what you face easier. I have to believe the circumstances of what you endured will factor in."

"You're not from around here, Reverend. No one is going to care that he hurt me. They'll just see me as violent. The judges and lawyers don't care about people like me."

"So, you did shoot him?"

Cecelia nodded. "And I'm not sorry. I don't know how he found me, but he showed up this morning. Dennis didn't know I'd taken Devon's gun with me when I left. I figured, if I had it, he couldn't use it on me. And he didn't. I'm going to jail, but he can't hurt me anymore."

Margot reached through the cell bars, gesturing for Cecelia to come closer. The other woman stayed put. "Cecelia, I'm so sorry, but the man you shot wasn't Devon. The police confirmed it was Dennis."

"No, they didn't. It was Devon. They found his ID on the body."

"They ran his fingerprints and it isn't Devon. I'm so sorry."

Cecelia's eyes widened to the size of saucers. "You mean he's still alive?"

"I'm afraid so. Do you have any idea why he might have wanted Dennis dead?"

"Their fight was huge, but it was Dennis who said he'd kill Devon if he laid a hand on me again. Devon was so wrapped up in his addiction, I don't think he really believed him."

"Gambling?" Margot posited.

"How'd you know?"

"It wasn't hard to find out he had a record and some outstanding warrants."

"You must think I'm a horrible person and I'm going to Hell."

"I don't. Not on either count. I think you made a mistake based on the circumstances you were trying to escape. I may be a minister, but I don't know that I believe in Hell. Not for people who are redeemable and you are, Cecelia. Please, can I help you get an attorney? One who will fight for you?"

Cecelia's eyes sparkled with unshed tears, but she nodded. "Okay. I don't know why you're being so nice to me."

"You deserve a second chance. And you have more people in your corner than you think. I'll be back."

"Where are you going?" Cecelia called as Margot started for the door.

"To find the last piece to this puzzle."

MARGOT STOOD on the front porch of Dennis' apartment and knocked. She wasn't sure he would still be there. Still if he'd seen the commotion surrounding Cecelia, he might have decided to stick around for just a little longer. He'd orchestrated all of this. He needed to pay for what he'd done. She knocked harder a second time. Still no reply, but when she tried the handle, the door swung inward. She wasn't normally reckless, but she could take care of herself. Her Army training had made sure of that. Besides, Devon wouldn't be the first person she subdued.

"Anyone home?" She called, crossing the threshold.

The apartment, much like Kalina had suspected earlier, was a mess. Clothing and drawers were strewn on the floor. She made her way deeper into the place, finding the bedroom at the back of the first floor. This was the most obvious sign of disruption. Hangers littered the room and a safe sat open on the floor, emptied of whatever had been inside. Given the gun case, Margot suspected Devon was once again armed. A phone sat charging on the nightstand by the bed.

Using a tissue to pick it up, she hit the power button. An image of who she assumed was Devon and Cecelia filled the screen. She swiped across the screen and the phone unlocked without a passcode. Navigating to recent texts, she found an exchange with Dennis from the night before.

Devon 11:28pm: Where are you? I don't want to leave things like we did. I want to say a real goodbye before you leave.

Dennis 11:31pm: Not interested.

Devon 11:32pm: Please, bro. I know I screwed up. I'm not like you. I got issues, but I want to be better. Please, man. You're going off to war and I don't know when I'm going to see you again.

Dennis 11:37pm: I'll think about it.

There was a five-hour gap in the messages.

Dennis 5:07am: I'll send you the address. But it has to be quick. I've got to head out soon.

Devon 5:12am: I'll be there.

Margot still wondered if Devon had known his girlfriend was in his brother's company when he'd headed over to the bed and breakfast that morning. Or had he been intending to kill his brother all along, and simply let Cecelia take the fall?

Margot left the bedroom in search of a baggie she could use to store the evidence, not wanting to disturb the scene any more than she already had. Just as she found a re-sealable plastic bag in the kitchen, a car door slammed out front. Margot pocketed the phone in the protective bag and pressed herself to the wall of the kitchen, attempting to stay out of sight. The front door opened with a boom as someone's foot connected with the wood.

"Find him," a baritone voice ordered, and

footsteps spread out upstairs and down the hall where Margot had just been.

She chanced a look into the front hall and spotted the slender man in the trench coat. "He's not here, boss," one of the men called from the back of the house.

"He's not dumb enough to ditch his phone."

"But you heard what the news lady said. He's dead."

"I'll be the judge of that," Trench Coat replied, sending chills down Margot's spine.

She prayed the phone didn't have a ringer on as he pressed his own device to his ear.

"You sure it's the right guy, Officer?" Trench Coat started to pace.

Margot's heart stopped. There were more than just a few officers in the Collingwood police force, but she knew of only one who'd had suspect dealings with Devon in the past.

Trench Coat hung up his call and snapped

his fingers. "Come on. Our friend says we can view the body at the morgue to be sure, but he ran his prints personally and it's our boy."

Margot waited until the men left the house before retreating herself. She needed to find Devon before those men realized he was still very much alive. They'd been tracking his phone, which explained how they'd ended up at his brother's apartment. It was only a matter of time before they found him.

Running through the small town invigorated Margot as she raced back to the bed and breakfast. The weight of the phone in her pocket was an ever-present reminder that if she didn't find Devon soon, they'd have another dead body on their hands. Kalina and Chris met her at the sidewalk as she skidded to a halt in the slush.

"I know why Cecelia did it. She thought she was killing Devon. We have bigger problems though, Devon's bookie is still looking for him," Margot announced, pulling the phone from her pocket. "I found this in Dennis' apartment. It's Devon's. I think Devon set up his brother to get killed. Goaded him into revealing where he was under the guise of reconciliation before Dennis deployed. His bookie was tracking his phone and they showed up before I left."

"We did some research of our own. It turns out Officer Johns was friends with Devon back in high school," Kalina said. "He's been giving him breaks on charges for years. We don't have any hard evidence, but I'd say Johns is protecting Devon."

"It would explain why he lied to his partner about who it was we found this morning. If Devon is in deep with a bookie, then faking his death is a surefire way to get out of debt," Margot added.

Chris' brow furrowed. "But he had to know they could find out he had a twin brother. I mean, even with limited resources we figured it out."

"The bookie isn't convinced, even though Johns is telling him the body is Devon. They're going to the morgue to check now."

"So, what do we do?" Kalina asked.

"Find Devon before they do," Margot answered.

"Any idea where he might go?" Chris interjected.

"If he's trying to assume Dennis' life, I'd have to guess he'd try to see Cecelia one last time."

"But she knows it's not Dennis," Kalina said.

Margot's heart ached for the turmoil surrounding Cecelia. "I think she's a very confused young woman who is still trying to process what she's done." Margot replied, gesturing toward the door. "Now, come on. We're wasting time."

OFFICER JOHNS WAS NOWHERE to be seen when they arrived at the station, and that made Margot nervous. She couldn't decide if that meant he had gone to meet Devon's bookie at the morgue or if he realized he'd been made and was trying to evade justice. Neither option instilled her with much confidence. Upon closer inspection, the station was oddly empty. There'd been at least a couple other officers on duty when Margot had come by to see Cecelia earlier. *Where'd they all go?* She didn't think her hunch about Devon's whereabouts was wrong. Although maybe she'd misjudged the amount of influence he had over the small police force?

"This seems too easy," Kalina whispered as they stood in the reception area.

"It does feel off," Chris agreed.

Chills ran down Margot's back that had nothing to do with the winter weather outside. "I don't disagree, but we need to hurry. If Devon knows his bookie is still looking for him, he may take even more drastic measures." She led Chris and Kalina to the holding area.

Devon stood before Cecelia in Dennis' dress blues. The sight of him turned Margot's stomach and her shoulders stiffened. *How dare he dishonor what the uniform stands for.* She could see Cecelia shaking under Devon's grip on her wrist.

"Let her go!" Chris yelled, his hands moving to his belt, no doubt reaching for a gun no longer holstered there.

Devon turned to face them, but he didn't let go of Cecelia's wrist.

"Devon, I know you're scared right now. But hurting Cecelia isn't going to make things better," Margot said, closing the distance.

"Stay back," he ordered, a handgun coming into view in his other hand.

Margot stopped short and held her hands out where he could see them. "I'm not going to come any closer, but I will ask you to let go of her. She's going to jail for killing your brother. Isn't that enough punishment?"

Devon relinquished his grip on Cecelia's arm. Immediately she shuffled backward, curling up on the bench in the far corner of the cell. Devon turned; he held the gun loosely in his grip.

"You're running. I think we can all see that. Can you tell us what happened?" Margot gestured to the two people behind her. "We all just want to understand how you got here. Can you help us?"

"He was always so much better than me. Better grades, better girlfriends ... Better ambitions. I didn't want to get pulled into this mess. It was supposed to be just a few bets. But it got out of control. I knew I could never pay it back. Not in the time I had. I knew the only way I'd get out of it is if everyone thought I was dead."

"You weren't worried they'd go after your friends and family?" Kalina asked.

"He has a code. Your debt is yours, no one else's," Devon answered, shifting his weight back and forth as if he couldn't decide the best direction to flee.

"So, you were trying to get out of debt, so the logical progression was to murder your brother and assume his identity?" Chris's tone carried a heavy dose of accusation.

Devon pivoted back to Cecelia, who cowered in the corner. "She wanted him instead of me. I could see it. So, I thought maybe if I was him, things would be okay."

"You had to know people would investigate," Margot said calmly, hoping her demeanor and tone of voice would keep him from lashing out.

"I told Johns that he might be getting a call about a dead body. He promised that he'd respond and take care of it. We go back a ways. He's always looked out for me."

"So, he was in on your plan to disappear under your brother's identity?"

Devon nodded. "It would have been perfect, too. I mean, people don't check fingerprints that often. I wouldn't even have to remember a new birthday or anything. I could be better than I was."

"I understand. But you have to know that you're going to jail for what you've done," Margot said.

Devon's gaze flickered from the gun in his hand to Margot and her companions. His hand trembled as he started to lift it.

"You have to know if you pull that trigger, you aren't getting out of here alive," Chris said.

Does he think Devon is going to shoot all of us to make his escape?

"I know," Devon sighed, turning the gun inward. "But it's not like people don't already think I'm a dead man."

Margot saw what was about to happen—

a desperate man about to end his own life— and lunged. Their bodies hit the floor with a thump and she used her own weight to pin him down.

His breath was hot against her face as she reached for the gun. Everything else fell away and slowed down. Except her and the deadly weapon in his hand. *Just a few more inches.* Her fingers stretched out and finally found purchase on the muzzle of the gun.

"No!" Kalina shouted as Margot finally freed the gun from Devon's grasp.

A shot rang out, deafening Margot's eardrums as she rolled off Devon. Panic sent her into overdrive. Her hands patted down her torso, but found no sign of injury. She turned to see Chris and Kalina standing side by side, their gazes turned upward. She followed their eyes to the ceiling where a single bullet sat lodged in the paneling. She'd gotten lucky.

Officers materialized as if out of thin air,

Officer Vargas among them. Two of them approached Devon, hauling him to his feet.

"I heard everything. After our discussion at the house, I thought he might show up so we let him think he had the upper hand," Officer Vargas explained before turning to address Devon. "You are charged with conspiracy to commit murder and identity theft. You have the right to remain silent. Anything you say can and will be used against you in a court of law," he said, administering the Miranda rights as they led Devon away.

"Please tell me you don't go charging men with guns often," Chris said, offering Margot a hand up.

"Sadly, more often than you'd think."

"Well, let's hope you don't have to do that again for a very long time."

By the following morning, news had broken about Devon's scheme, and how Devon had been aided by Officer Johns. Both were now in custody and Margot had reached out to a lawyer friend who agreed to take Cecelia's case pro bono.

Margot sat outside on the front porch of the B&B, enjoying the morning stillness. Kalina joined her, offering a mug of hot chocolate.

"I think Caroline may have spiked it … just a little," Kalina said with a small smirk.

Margot returned the smile. "Everything in moderation, right?" She took a sip, tasting the tiniest hint of alcohol in the froth. Given what had transpired she was grateful for the bit of numbness it provided.

Kalina tucked her legs under her in the seat and looked at Margot. "You were really impressive yesterday, talking Devon down."

"I've had practice and training. I went overseas to serve God but that didn't mean I never had to defend myself or others while in the line of duty." She used her mug to gesture back to Kalina. "From the things you've said, it's not completely out of your realm of experience either."

"I wanted to confront him," Kalina said and her tone went breathy, "but it was like I was frozen in place. I saw the gun and I immediately thought about my daughter. How if I did or said the wrong thing, I could lose her."

"That's the rational response. You put

your child first. It's a biological imperative," Margot replied.

"Not a godly one though?" Kalina's slender brow arched upward.

"Well, He made us, so I suppose yes it's His imperative, too." Margot's right hand brushed against the cross at her neck. *Thank you for seeing us all through another crisis.*

A peaceful silence fell between them. Kalina took a long pull from her mug and after a moment, she spoke. "So, what will you do now that everything has died down?"

"Go home. Share our crazy story with my cousin, Sam. Pray that Cecelia will be given the fair trial she deserves and that she can start to heal."

"How do you heal from something like this?" Kalina asked.

"With time and people to listen. Even if she serves time, I hope she's able to get some therapy. To build herself back up after everything Devon put her through."

"I get the feeling she'll be able to do that. Besides, she's got you looking out for her."

Margot smiled, but said nothing. All she'd done was make a couple of phone calls. She wasn't a miracle worker. Now it was up to Cecelia to put in the work.

"I hope Officer Johns gets what he deserves, too," Kalina said softly, a slight edge to her tone.

Her comment reminded Margot of something Kalina had said the day before. She hadn't had time to follow up on it in the midst of chasing down Devon. "Yesterday, you said something about knowing that good people can do bad things for the right reason. It sounded personal."

Kalina studied the contents of her mug. "The first case I worked with Chris ... was when we reconnected. The Chief of Police turned out to be the son of a man wrongfully convicted of murder. He was seeking revenge against the three witnesses who'd put his father in prison."

"How awful." Margot reached over and put a hand on Kalina's shoulder. "I can see how that would be upsetting."

"It worked out then, and it's worked out now, too. The bad guys have been caught and justice done. Maybe now we can go home and not have to solve a murder for a while."

That sounded lovely. Margot couldn't wait to get back to Port Marie and the normalcy of tending to her congregation. It's what she did best.

As she reflected on her New Year's excitement, she realized that Devon and Dennis' story was as old as Biblical tales. After all, Cain and Abel had been loving brothers once, turned against one another by emotions they perhaps didn't understand. Had Dennis felt responsible for his brother's bad actions? Devon's jealousy had certainly led him astray. And just like Cain, he would pay for his jealousy for the rest of his life. Margot could only hope that he would eventually see the error of his ways and work to make better choices in the future.

LOVE THY NEIGHBOR

A REVEREND MARGOT QUADE
COZY MYSTERY NOVELLA BOOK 5

S.E. BIGLOW

LOVE THY NEIGHBOR Copyright © 2019 by Sarah Biglow.

For information contact; www.sarah-biglow.com

Copyedited by: Liza Street

Proofreading and formatting by: Under Wraps Publishing Services

Cover Design by: Deranged Doctor Design

Published by Sarah Biglow: August 2020

10 9 8 7 6 5 4 3 2 1

 Created with Vellum

1

In the eighteen months since Margot's homecoming, the small town had finally settled into a new normal. She and her cousin Sam even had a stronger bond than when she'd left for the Middle East, and the interfaith worship space was bustling more than ever.

Even though it wasn't required, Margot often attended the other services just to see her colleagues work. She found their varying expressions of faith comforting. They might say different prayers or speak in other languages, but they all gave thanks to a creator who saw the inherent goodness in humanity.

After a Muslim service, Margot stood on the front steps as three hijabi women passed by her into the warm March air.

"Hello, Reverend," Amira Fayet, the youngest of the three, said when she spotted Margot.

"Hi, Amira," Margot replied. "How are your college applications going?"

Amira's vibrant face fell a little and she cast a glance at the other women with whom she walked. They appeared deep in a conversation of their own, so Amira stepped closer to Margot. "My parents don't want me to leave town for school. They are worried about what might happen."

Her fingertips brushed the delicate fabric framing her face.

"I can understand their fear," Margot said.

"The world we live in isn't as kind as it should be. But you're a smart girl. I'm sure you'll find your way to where you're supposed to be." After a pause, Margot asked, "Will I see you tomorrow for brunch?"

"I think so." Amira gave a tight-lipped smile and nod before her mother noticed that she wasn't at her side and beckoned her back.

Amira's parents didn't know that their daughter was one of the co-founders of the interfaith youth group at the church. From what Amira had shared, her parents were devout in their faith to the point of excluding all others. Margot got the sense they weren't thrilled they had to share a worship space with Christians and Jews.

Margot's phone buzzed in her pocket and she looked to see an incoming call from Sam. Answering, Margot said, "Hey, don't tell me you have to cancel dinner."

"No, I'm stuck at the station writing up reports so just going to be running late," Sam said.

Her cousin's statement seemed a little odd. Margot didn't remember her being on shift today, but maybe she'd gotten her cousin's schedule wrong.

"Just let me know when you're free," Margot said. "I can always grab take-out and bring it to you."

"Thanks. I'll let you know."

Sam ended the call and Margot stowed her phone. She and Sam were getting dinner for a reason. Sam had generously offered to help Margot move into her new place, and this was Margot's preemptive thank you. Although, the new place wasn't entirely new. In fact, it had been church property for over sixty years. Margot had resisted moving into the parsonage for long enough. She wasn't planning to go anywhere, so it made sense to take up residence in the space the church had specifically set aside for her.

With the unseasonably warm weather, she decided to make the short walk to the parsonage, winding along the front of the church. So much had happened since she'd come home and much of it painful, but ultimately healing. She was grateful the last few months in Port Marie had been quiet and peaceful as the world around them signaled new life and rebirth.

"Afternoon, Margot," a familiar voice called to her just as she reached her destination's driveway.

Moses Davidson—another of the youth leaders—approached from the sidewalk. He wore a navy hoodie with a Star of David embroidered on the breast. Just below it sat the symbols for the other faiths that were celebrated within the interfaith space. He'd lobbied the youth group to get some sort of branding. He was going to be a marketing major in college.

"Moses, how are you?" She said and pulled the young man into a brief, one-armed hug.

"I'm all right. I didn't get a chance to tell you yet, but I got accepted to American University," he said, beaming. The clear excitement made his caramel-colored eyes shine.

"That's fantastic. Your parents must be so proud," Margot said.

Much like her conversation with Amira only minutes earlier, the mention of his parents dampened his mood. "They want me to stay closer to home. They think D.C. is too far away. They'd think anything is too far away."

He tugged on the chain around his neck with the tiny Star of David pendant, the outward symbol of his own faith.

"Whatever you decide to do, I know it will be the right move for you. Will I see you at the youth group brunch tomorrow?" Margot gave him a sympathetic look.

"Wouldn't miss it," Moses said, brightening again.

"Great. You know, I love watching you, Amira, and Cameron work together so seamlessly. You have such respect for each other and embrace the common ground between yourselves. I wish everyone had the same kindness in their hearts as you three." She thought they were probably so close, because they'd all grown up as neighbors.

He averted his gaze for a moment before returning his focus to her. "Cam would be blushing so hard right now if he heard you say that about him. But, thanks. Fellowship is supposed to be about supporting your fellow man."

"Exactly."

He checked his phone. "I, uh, gotta be somewhere. See you later." He gave her a wave and darted back up the street in the direction he'd come.

Margot couldn't help smiling to herself as she strode up to the front of her new home. She'd never had so much space to herself before. The house boasted two full bathrooms, three bedrooms, a living room, a kitchen, and a fully furnished basement. She barely had enough belongings to her name to fill her bedroom and the living room. Entering the kitchen, she sensed a disruption to the stillness. Time in the military had made her hypersensitive to her surroundings most of the time, especially if she wasn't yet comfortable in the space—like now.

She was not alone.

Her hands balled into fists as she pressed herself along the wall that led to the living room. She caught fabric rustling out of the corner of her eye. *The windows weren't open.* She slipped into the next room, her right hand searching for the light switch. Even though the ambient light from outside was decent, it was reflex.

Light flooded the room and she staggered back as a group led by Sam and Patrick Hawley jumped out.

"Surprise!" a chorus of voices echoed in the confined space.

She spotted Amira among the group. Cameron Henderson stood beside her with a giant grin on his face. It hadn't been a coincidence she'd run into both Amira and Moses on her way here. They'd purposely sought her out to stall her. Obviously, that averted look Moses had done and the message on his phone must have been a signal from one of the other kids that it was okay to let Margot inside.

Margot's heart hammered in her chest as she studied the people standing in her living room.

"You okay?" Sam asked, slinging an arm around Margot's shoulders.

"What is all this?" Margot asked, trying to regulate her heart rate and her breathing.

"I know you don't like surprises. I swear it wasn't my idea. Blame those three over there," Sam answered, pointing to Cameron, Amira, and Moses all of them looking slightly out of breath.

"But Sam, I'm not even fully moved in. There are whole rooms that have nothing in them," Margot protested.

Without a word, Sam grabbed her arm and led her upstairs. They stopped at the first door on the right. She gestured for Margot to open the door. Margot pressed her fingertips to the painted wood and gave it a gentle push. The door opened to reveal a fully furnished—and tastefully so, if Margot was being honest—bedroom.

"You did all of this?" Margot whispered as Sam led her down the hall to see the other two bedrooms, one of which had been turned into a home office. A simple desk with office chair sat below a framed photo of Sam and Margot just taken the prior summer.

"I knew you'd feel out of place in a big house by yourself with just your own stuff. So, we figured we'd make it feel more like a home."

Margot pulled her cousin into a tight embrace. "Thank you. I can't put into words how much this means to me. Even if I don't like surprises."

"Oh, you haven't seen the best part yet."

Sam barreled down the stairs to the first floor and stared up at Margot from the landing. For a moment, remembered her as the young teenage girl who'd spent so much time with Margot while they were growing up. They'd been as close as sisters. Time and different paths had driven them apart for a while, but they'd found their way back to each other.

"You coming?" Sam called.

Margot gave her a grin and headed down to the first floor at a more dignified pace before she and Sam made their way to the basement. She wasn't sure what to expect from the room, but the moment she set foot on soft carpeting, she knew it was perfect. One wall was lined with books and cozy reading chairs. The other side offered up space for prayer, complete with beautifully-made prayer rugs.

"Was this you?" Margot asked and nudged Sam's shoulder.

"I'd love to take the credit, but again, it was the kids. I think maybe they wanted a place away from their parents where they could spend time together."

"But they already have the interfaith space and its perfect for them," Margot pointed out.

"I think they feel safer with you around," Sam said.

"I'm glad I make them feel safe, but I'm

not sure my basement is the best place for them to be hanging out," Margot noted.

"Well, there are some people who are still a little uncomfortable going down to the church basement after what happened with Conrad Baptiste," Sam replied.

"I can understand that. Okay, fine. I'll have to set some limits. Besides I suppose it's only for a few months at least until they're all off to school."

Footsteps thundered down the stairs before Cameron and Moses staggered into the space, laughing. Amira appeared behind them, giving Margot an eye roll at her friends' antics.

"So, I hear all of this was your idea," Margot said.

Amira ducked her head in embarrassment, while Cameron and Moses stood tall and grinned ear to ear.

"It's really cool, right?" Cameron said.

Margot nodded and smiled at them all. "I

appreciate your thoughtfulness. But I think we're going to need to lay down some ground rules about being here. This is my house, after all, and I can't have people coming and going any time they want."

"We know, Reverend," Amira said softly.

"After school is fine … after services, too. But you're not going to skip school or stay here late," Margot said, her tone firm.

"Yes, ma'am," Moses answered.

"Thanks, Rev," Cameron said.

"Now, this is a party, so I'm guessing someone brought food? How about we eat?" Margot suggested.

The three teens raced back up the stairs and Sam started to follow them. Margot hung back in the basement for a minute longer, letting the stillness of the space calm her nerves. She could see herself spending a lot of time down here.

Knowing it was rude for the guest of honor to be absent from the party, Margot returned to the first floor. The front and back doors, along with the living room windows, had been opened to the warm evening air. Someone handed her a plate with a mixture of cheese, crackers, and hummus. She turned to see Reverend Hawley standing beside her.

"This place is going to suit you beautifully," he said.

"Does it feel strange not to live here anymore? To see it so totally transformed?" She nibbled on a cracker.

"I always knew this wasn't going to be my permanent home. It was meant for someone else. Someone who was going to stay here for a long time."

"I appreciate your confidence in my ministry," she noted.

"Have you seen the basement?"

"It's lovely."

"We had to talk the boys out of putting in a ping-pong table."

Margot snorted, the food on her plate shifting precariously close to the edge. "That does seem like something the two of them would insist on. Let me guess, Amira reminded them it wasn't a good idea."

"Exactly. I hope the three of them remain friends even after they graduate and move away."

"I'm not sure they're all going to be moving away. It sounds like both Amira's and Moses' parents don't want them going far from Port Marie. I haven't talked to Cameron, but I always got the feeling he didn't have an interest in leaving town, either."

Before Reverend Hawley could speak, a scream echoed from the front of the house. Margot didn't think, she just reacted. The plate in her hand fell to the floor and she reached the front of the house in under thirty seconds.

Amira stood in the doorway with her

hands pressed over her mouth to muffle more screams. Her father lay sprawled on the grass in front of the parsonage. He clutched his chest and his entire body spasmed.

2

"Sam!" Margot bellowed as she pushed past the girl and fell to her knees on the grass.

Sam appeared and was at Margot's side, retrieving her phone to call 9-1-1. Margot kept her focus on Amira's father.

"It's going to be okay," Margot said. "Can you tell me what is happening?"

"I … my chest hurts," he rasped, slurring his words as he reached a hand out to her.

He must have been in a lot of pain and disoriented, because in the time she'd known him, he'd never shaken her hand or otherwise touched another woman's hand besides his wife's or his daughter's.

"It sounds like you might be having a heart attack. The paramedics are on their way," Sam said just as sirens whined in the distance. Red and white lights strobed across the front of the house.

"Daddy," Amira cried and tried to squeeze herself in at his side.

"Amira, I know you're really scared right now, but you need to back up and let them work," Margot said, releasing her grip on the man's hand and focusing her attention on restraining his daughter.

The medics climbed from the ambulance and busied themselves tending to Amira's father. Tears streamed down Amira's face and sobs shook her body as Margot held tight to her.

"Come on, let's go back inside," Margot whispered.

"He needs me," Amira whimpered.

"The best thing you can do for your father right now is to let them work. They're going to take him to the hospital. Let's call your mother and let her know what's happened. I'll take you to the hospital myself."

"Thank you," Amira sniffled.

Margot ushered Amira back inside the house and found Reverend Hawley. "I'm afraid the party is over. If you wouldn't mind asking everyone to leave, I'd appreciate it. Amira needs some support right now."

"Of course." Reverend Hawley turned to face the group. Most of them hadn't gone rushing out to see what had happened after Amira screamed. Maybe they had just assumed it was in good hands.

"Everyone, I'm sorry to say the festivities need to wrap up. If you all wouldn't mind pitching in to clean up so Reverend Quade has a nice clean home when she comes back, it would be much appreciated."

Moses and Cameron appeared at Amira's side. "What's going on?" Moses asked.

"My father ..." Amira broke down in fresh tears.

"Is he okay?" Moses pressed, pulling Amira into a tight hug. She shook her head and buried her face in his shoulder.

Cameron stood off to the side for a moment before joining in the group hug. The boys led Amira down toward the basement. Behind Margot, she heard footsteps and turned to see Sam.

"They're taking him to the hospital now," Sam said. "Has anyone let his wife know?"

Margot said, "Amira's going to call her mother when she's calmed down."

Sam nodded her head toward the back of the house and Margot followed her cousin out to the tidy, fenced-in backyard.

"He didn't seem like the type to have a heart attack," Sam said.

"We don't know anything about his medical history," Margot countered.

"I noticed some weird patches of skin on his left arm. Like a rash."

"Sam, what are you doing?" Margot turned to face her cousin.

"Nothing, just noting some odd things with how his symptoms presented."

"You aren't a doctor and neither am I."

"No, but something just feels a little odd."

"I'm sure you're reading too much into this." Although Margot had an idea of why Sam might be fishing for a case. Things had been calm in Port Marie for a long while now. She had a feeling her cousin now found her job a little boring. It lacked the excitement of a murder or a kidnapping.

"Maybe you're right," Sam said.

"I'm going to take Amira to the hospital and make sure she calls her mother."

Sam squeezed Margot's hand before letting go. "Keep me in the loop."

PULLING Amira away from her friends took some doing. The boys wanted to join her at the hospital. Though Margot pointed out that for the time being, this was a family matter. They could be good friends once they had a better idea of what was going on.

As Margot and Amira walked back to the church to retrieve her car, Margot considered Sam's statements. She didn't want to believe there was something amiss in Mr. Fayet's symptoms. Still Margot couldn't deny there was a small piece of her that missed the chase of solving a case with her cousin, too. *A few questions wouldn't hurt.*

"Amira, has your father been having any health problems that you know of?" Margot tried not to sound too much like an interrogator.

"No. He's healthy. He eats right and exercises all the time." Amira's voice was stronger than when they'd left the parsonage.

"I'm sure he'll be okay then since he's healthy," Margot said.

"I don't know why he was coming to the party. He had refused to go," Amira noted softly.

"You can ask him when he gets settled," Margot suggested as they climbed into her car. "Now, call your mother and let her know what's going on."

Amira dialed her home number. It would be a five-minute trip to the hospital. Fresh tears welled up in Amira's eyes as she waited for her mother to answer. The phone was on speaker as Margot pulled up to the one stop light between them and their destination.

"Amira? Is everything all right? Are you coming home?" Her mother's voice sounded louder than it should over the connection.

"No, I'm going to the hospital. Daddy …

they took him in an ambulance." Her words devolved into a sob, obscuring her last word.

"What?"

"He's at the hospital. They think he had a heart attack," Amira sniffled.

"Are you with someone safe?"

Margot cleared her throat. "Mrs. Fayet, it's Margot Quade. I'm going to wait with Amira until you arrive."

"Thank you," Mrs. Fayet said, and Amira ended the call.

The rest of the drive went quickly. Margot pulled into the parking lot of the hospital and stopped in the first non-handicap spot by the Emergency Room's entrance.

Amira stumbled out of the car before Margot had even pulled the key from the ignition. Margot yanked the keys free and raced after the girl. They likely hadn't beaten the ambulance here, but even so, the doctors wouldn't yet have a good idea of what had happened to Mr. Fayet.

Amira rushed to the central desk and waved her hands. "My father. Where's my father?"

"Miss, you need to calm down," a nurse in pale purple scrubs told Amira.

Margot stepped up and wrapped an arm around the girl's shoulders before guiding her to a chair out of the way. "I know this is a scary time, but you need to let the doctors do what they're trained to do."

"I just don't understand why he got sick," she said, worrying her hands in her lap.

"They're going to find out what's going on," Margot said and patted her knee. They fell into silence for a while as people ebbed and flowed from rooms and areas of the Emergency Department.

"Amira!" Mrs. Fayet called as she burst through the doors of the ER. Her voice disrupted the strained silence.

Amira stood at the sight of her mother

and flung herself into her arms. They stood together and as Margot watched the exchange, she was reminded just how young Amira really was. Margot bowed her head and said a small prayer for Mr. Fayet's recovery. He may not approve of other religions, but she doubted even he would refuse good thoughts on his behalf especially in his current condition.

"Mrs. Fayet?" A doctor in blue scrubs appeared from a doorway and stepped into the waiting area.

Amira and her mother separated, both turned to look at the doctor.

"Yes? What has happened to my husband?" Mrs. Fayet demanded.

"Why don't we go somewhere and talk privately." The doctor's pointed look at Margot suggested she wasn't invited for the family meeting.

"Please let me know if there's anything I can do," Margot said to Mrs. Fayet.

Mrs. Fayet glanced from her daughter to Margot and back again. "Thank you for staying with her and for bringing her here."

"She helped Daddy," Amira added. "She was the first person to go to him."

Margot's phone buzzed in her pocket and she excused herself to let the family speak with the doctor. Sam's face flashed on her screen. "Hey Sam."

"What's the latest?"

"I don't know. Amira's mother just got here and they're speaking with the doctor now. I can't see why I should stick around. I'm not really who they'd turn to in a crisis."

"Maybe not Mrs. Fayet, but Amira will need you. She may be Muslim, but she sees you as a mentor and a shoulder to lean on."

"You still think something weird is going on?"

"I don't know. Maybe."

"If they tell me anything and it sounds

suspicious, I can pass it along," Margot offered.

"Thanks. Oh, and don't worry about the house. It's all cleaned up."

"Thank you."

Margot ended the call and started for the exit when someone's hand reached out and touched her arm. She turned to find the charge nurse, a grey-haired woman in her sixties, gesturing for her to step closer.

"What is it?" Margot asked quietly.

"I know it's not my business … and it's not very godly to be nosy, but the man they just brought in didn't look good. I heard them say they might have to induce a coma."

"I thought he had a heart attack?" Margot whispered.

"Maybe, but it also sounds like he might've had a massive stroke."

Margot studied the woman's face, crow's feet crinkled at the corners of her eyes. "Why are you telling me this?"

She cocked her head to one side and gave Margot an exasperated look. "Port Marie is a small town, Reverend. It's not a secret you were at the heart of a lot of the heart-breaking things that came up in the last year and a half. It seems like whenever the town is in need of some healing, you're somehow in the middle of it. If this is another of those times, well all I can say is, I hope you can figure out what happened."

Margot studied the nurse in stunned si-lence. Yes, she'd been involved in solving a few cases that had rocked Port Marie. Still she didn't seek them out. She happened upon them by accident or happenstance. Even then she was always working with Sam on those cases. But Sam had been pushing her to think that Mr. Fayet's condition was something other than a normal illness. Did Sam miss working together? *Maybe I miss it, too.*

Before Margot could react to the nurse's

statement, Amira went running by out into the parking lot, the back of her hijab flying out behind her in a flurry of fabric. After a beat, when her mother didn't appear, Margot took off after the girl. She found her sitting on a bench, knees pressed to her chest and her face buried against her legs.

"What's wrong? What did the doctor say?" Margot coaxed.

"They said it wasn't a heart attack. It was a stroke, but something went wrong. He started having trouble breathing and they said he had a seizure. He's in a medically-induced coma. They don't know if he will wake up." The words spilled out of Amira's mouth like they had no choice, but to come out.

"Your dad is strong and a fighter. Don't give up on him. He's going to need you to be strong while he recovers," Margot said and squeezed the girl's hand.

"What if it's a sign from Allah?" Amira whispered.

"What do you mean?"

Amira studied her hands. "Daddy didn't want me to go away to school. What if Allah doesn't, either? What if he made Daddy sick for a reason?"

"Amira, I know we practice our faith differently, but I cannot believe that your god is a vengeful or punishing god. You are an intelligent young woman with a wonderful future. If anything, I believe God would want to see you succeed in whatever you set your mind to."

The automatic doors to the ER slid open and Mrs. Fayet stepped out, looking around. She met Margot's gaze and tugged her hijab closer around her face.

Margot was already on her feet by the time the woman reached the bench. "Mrs. Fayet, if there is anything I or the other faith leaders can do to support your family, please let me know."

Given Amira's emotional response, Margot expected her mother to be equally concerned. Instead, her eyes were dry and in fact, there was no evidence she'd shed a tear at all. Perhaps she was trying to put on a strong front for her daughter. Margot couldn't believe that there was anything sinister beneath the woman's calm exterior.

"We have our own community to rely upon. We've had enough trouble from other people," she finally said.

"Of course," Margot replied before giving Amira one last hand squeeze.

She watched mother and daughter disappear toward the far end of the parking lot. She hadn't expected Mrs. Fayet to accept her offer of support. Although the way she'd just ushered Amira away, not even going back to sit vigil at her husband's side, was perplexing.

Margot retrieved her phone and called Sam back. It rang three times before her cousin answered.

"Was I right?" Sam sounded so hopeful.

"I'm not sure," Margot said slowly. She was still puzzling it out in her own mind. "Mrs. Fayet is acting strange though. Rather than stay with her husband, she left with Amira. She said they'd had enough trouble from other people when I offered ministerial support. It's probably nothing, but maybe you could check to see if Mr. Fayet had any issues with anyone in town?"

"Give me a second." Margot heard the clicking of computer keys as Sam typed. The clicking stopped suddenly, and Sam was silent.

"What is it?" Margot asked.

"I think…you might want to come down to the precinct."

Dread settled in Margot's stomach as she ended the call and retreated to her car.

3

Despite her best efforts, Margot failed to keep her worst-case scenario from flashing through her mind. Had someone targeted Mr. Fayet, because of his faith? She wanted to believe Port Marie was different, that people of different faiths—or no faith at all—could live in peace. It was the very foundation of the interfaith worship space. Besides if there was someone out there targeting members of the community because of their religion, the small town would be on the brink of disaster before they knew it.

She found Sam sifting through several pages of computer print-outs on her desk.

"Please tell me whatever you found isn't as terrible as my mind is trying to convince me it is," Margot said in a whisper so the officers nearby wouldn't overhear her. There wasn't actually a case to be investigated yet, and she didn't want to start the rumor mill turning.

"I've got two years' worth of complaints between the Fayets and the Davidsons," Sam answered.

"You're sure?" Margot wasn't at an angle where she could read the details on the paper.

Sam nodded, her dark hair falling across her face. "It looks like it started with Mr. Davidson filing noise complaints about the early morning call to prayer."

Margot shook her head. "That's ridiculous. The call to prayer is a part of their religion. You can't keep someone from practicing their religion in their own home."

"That's exactly what the responding officer said. However, it didn't stop Davidson from filing other complaints after that. Petty things like parking on the street abutting their property. Then the Fayets started filing complaints back about encroaching on their property. They said the Davidsons were purposely doing things like mowing the lawn at times when the Fayets were trying to sleep."

"I just can't believe this is real," Margot said.

Sam fixed Margot with an incredulous look. "Even religious people can be jerks to each other. I thought you knew that."

Margot sank into the chair beside Sam's desk. "I know. I guess I was just hoping that cooler heads would prevail. Even petty complaints seem like a big leap from causing lasting physical harm."

"What's the latest?" Sam still didn't know about Mr. Fayet's condition.

"It seems he had a stroke with some complications. He's in a medically-induced coma," Margot answered.

"Maybe you're right and this isn't connected," Sam said, "but I won't know until I ask. And you should come along, too. I know the Fayets aren't exactly fond of you, but last I checked Mr. and Mrs. Davidson liked you."

The part of Margot that liked the thrill of solving a mystery threatened to take over as Sam scooped up the pages and headed for the parking lot. They still didn't know if there was a crime to look into. Amira might have assumed her father was healthy, but parents didn't always tell their children everything either.

"Promise me you won't push too hard? The family is dealing with a devastating situation," Margot reminded her cousin.

"I know that." Sam held up one of the

sheets of paper. "The last complaint was from a couple of weeks ago. I'm just doing my job and following up to make sure everything is fine."

EVEN BEING a half block away they could hear the shouting with the windows closed. Sam pressed hard on the accelerator and the car shot forward. Mrs. Fayet stood at the end of her driveway, gesturing wildly at Mr. Davidson.

"You did something to him," she screamed.

"I don't know what you're talking about," he answered.

Mrs. Fayet stepped closer, her finger mere inches from Mr. Davidson's face. "You make all these complaints to the police about us. You expect me to believe you didn't do something to him?"

"Mrs. Fayet, what's going on here?" Sam intervened, having bolted from the car as soon as the car stopped moving.

Margot was right behind her, scanning the area for signs of Moses or Amira. Neither appeared to be around despite the fact Margot had seen Amira leave with her mother only a short time ago.

"My husband is sick and in a coma. He was fine this morning."

Sam placed a hand on Mrs. Fayet's arm and forcefully turned her toward her own house. "Why don't you and I talk inside? There's no need to cause a scene."

Mrs. Fayet glared back at her neighbor who stood on the sidewalk, mouth agape.

Margot approached him. "Are you all right, Mr. Davidson?"

"What's she talking about? What happened to Hassan?"

"Maybe it's better if we go inside, too," Margot suggested. They didn't need to have such a personal conversation out in the open.

He gestured for her to go ahead of him up the short driveway and into the house. She hadn't been inside the home until recently, when the family had celebrated Passover. Moses had insisted she join them. She'd loved getting to observe the way the family celebrated and they'd been welcoming to her. This time, Mr. Davidson led Margot directly to the kitchen and put a kettle on the stove.

"Please, what happened to Hassan?" He asked.

"I'm assuming you knew about the surprise housewarming party Moses, Amira, and Cameron helped organize at the parsonage," Margot began.

"Of course. Moses was very excited."

"Well, Hassan showed up and collapsed. It looked like he might have been having a cardiac event. Only the doctors told Mrs. Fayet he'd suffered a stroke and they had to induce a coma."

"My Lord," he rasped, hand clasped over his mouth.

"I understand you've had some issues with Mr. Fayet recently," Margot said, letting him decide how much information he was willing to divulge.

"I know I shouldn't have complained, but I work late. By the time I get home, I just want to go to sleep. Their call to prayer was so loud."

"But you can't stop them from worshipping in their way," Margot reminded him.

"I know. I didn't mean for them not to use it. Just to make it a little quieter. I don't know how it wasn't waking half the neighborhood."

"It sounds like you haven't been getting along ever since," Margot noted as the kettle let out a shrill whistle.

"I'm at fault for much of that. I've prayed

about my part in all of this, sought forgiveness and guidance on how to make amends. But I can't be the only one trying to mend things. They have to be willing to see reason ... and they can't. I hate to say it, but I don't think they like how much time Moses and Amira spend together."

Was there a romantic interest there that Margot had missed? Every time she saw them, it was always a trio, not a duo. "What makes you say that?"

"I don't know if Amira realizes this, but Moses cares for her deeply. He's confided in me that he has feelings for her, but he knows they can never act on them."

"Because he's not Muslim," Margot said.

"Yes. Don't get me wrong, Reverend. I like Amira very much, but I know that if my son were to try and start some sort of relationship, rejection would break his heart. I would not wish that upon anyone's child. Now, I don't know what Mrs. Fayet thinks I could have done to her husband, but I assure you I haven't seen him in days. Not since the last complaint he filed with the police about where we tossed our snow after the last storm."

"Are you sure there've never been harsh words exchanged? Anything that could be interpreted as at all threatening?"

"Not that I can remember," he said and offered her a cup of tea.

"Thank you."

She sipped the tea, taking note of the flowery scent. "Is that lavender?"

"Yes. Rebecca buys it from the coffee shop on Main Street. They make it themselves. She gets it every morning. They gave her a few bags of leaves for Chanukah as a gift."

Margot's phone buzzed in her pocket. No doubt a message from Sam requesting a rendezvous to see what she'd learned.

Even if Mrs. Fayet believed that Mr.

Davidson had somehow found a way to harm her husband, Margot didn't see any evidence of such a crime. They were certainly at odds with one another over religion and the relationship shared by their children. Still that was hardly enough to lead someone to cause serious bodily harm to another person.

Or was it?

She'd witnessed people inflict harm on those they claimed to care about for a number of reasons that made little sense to her. Even if the harm had come from what the person believed to be a place of good intent. Warren Nesbit came to mind. He'd been her mystery to solve. His wife had doubled his insulin dose out of a desire to be needed again. "Well, thank you for the hospitality. Maybe you should give Mrs. Fayet a little space to collect herself, and I'm sure it will all work out."

"I doubt she'd accept my well wishes, but pass them on all the same, would you?"

"Of course."

Margot set the teacup down on the counter and showed herself out. Sam waited in the car with a scowl on her face. She stayed silent as she put the car in gear and pulled into the Davidson driveway to turn around.

"She seriously thinks he poisoned her husband," she finally said once they were headed back to the precinct.

"Does she have any idea how he might have achieved that?"

"Nope. Just kept insisting he'd done it, because he hates her family."

"That's not the story I got from Mr. Davidson. He feels guilty about calling in the noise complaint about their prayers. He just wanted them to be quieter. Things escalated from there. He also told me that Moses has a crush on Amira."

"Well, yeah. Anyone with eyes could see that," Sam snorted.

"I guess I'm blind, then," Margot muttered.

"You see the three of them in a controlled environment. I've seen just the two of them studying at the library. Hanging out downtown on weekends."

"So, Amira knows how Moses feels about her."

"I'd say the feeling's mutual."

"People have done far worse things for less reason than wanting to keep their children apart."

Sam pulled hard on the wheel and the tires skidded on the pavement as she made a sharp turn away from the precinct. "Mrs. Fayet thinks a crime's been committed. She said she's going to file a police report. I need to talk to the doctor and see what I can find out."

"I still don't see her being right," Margot said.

"And that's why it's called an investigation. We dig until we find the truth. If it isn't what she thinks it is, at least she'll have answers," Sam said and pulled into one of the available spaces in the hospital parking lot.

"Did you see Amira when you were talking to Mrs. Fayet?" Margot asked as they walked through the automatic double doors.

"No," Sam answered and stepped up to the nurse's station to ask for Mr. Fayet's room number.

They took the elevator to the second floor—the intensive care unit—and donned gloves and face masks at the nurse's direction before entering the room.

Amira sat by her father's bedside with her head bowed.

"Amira," Margot said softly, rousing the girl.

The girl looked up and the red rims

around her eyes signaled how much she'd been crying. "Did you talk to my mother?"

Sam stepped up and pulled over a chair. "We did. Do you know why she might think Mr. Davidson did something to your father?"

"She doesn't like Moses, because he's not Muslim. But Mr. Davidson is a nice man. He'd never hurt Daddy."

"Did you know there were complaints filed with the police between Mr. Davidson and your father?"

Margot bit her lip to keep quiet. Amira was over sixteen, but it still felt wrong to interview her without her mother present. Still, she understood Sam's reasoning. Amira was more likely to open up without her mother's watchful gaze.

"Yes, I knew," Amira answered softly.

"Had you noticed any changes in your father lately? Moodiness, things like that?" Sam pressed.

"No, nothing. He was fine. I mean, he

probably should cut back on the amount of coffee he drinks, but everyone says that."

"Did your father get his coffee from the shop on Main Street?" Margot interjected.

"Every morning. And I always bought him a couple pounds of their specialty blend for his birthday," Amira answered.

Margot pressed down on Sam's shoulder, hoping her cousin would understand the signal for what it was. She needed to share the scenario that had popped into her mind.

"If you think of anything else, call me, okay?" Sam said and patted Amira's forearm.

They stepped from the room and pulled off their protective gear. "Mrs. Davidson buys specialty tea from the same coffee shop," Margot whispered.

"You think if something happened it could have happened there?"

"Maybe. It feels like more than just a co-incidence that they both buy from the shop."

"It's worth checking out. But I still need

to follow up with the doctor to get a better picture of his prognosis and what exactly happened."

Margot left her cousin to dig into Mr. Fayet's medical situation. She had a date with a coffee.

Henderson Coffee was one of the busiest spots in Port Marie. Situated right at the center of town, everyone frequented it, even if they weren't a coffee or tea connoisseur. There was no doubt that someone they knew was and would appreciate some specialty brew or a gift certificate at holidays and birthdays.

Margot walked through the front door and let the mixture of aromas wash over her. There was the pungent, earthy scent of coffee beans going through the grinder and the sweeter hints of teas like mint, lavender, and chamomile. The walls were paneled in welcoming wooden hues and the counter boasted freshly baked breads and croissants that made Margot's mouth water. She'd barely eaten anything at the housewarming, and her stomach rumbled as a reminder.

"Can I help you, Reverend?" A young woman with bright pink braids asked.

Margot's hand instinctively moved to her neck where the cross and her dog tags hung, announcing her title before she even opened her mouth. Margot studied the girl behind the counter, her eyes widening as she realized she knew the woman. Casey Maddox had been in the children's choir when Margot had gone off to seminary.

"Hi, Casey. How are you?'

"I'm all right. Can I get you something to drink or eat?"

"You know, I'd love a couple of those croissants. Chocolate if you have them."

Casey slid the back of the display tray open and pulled out two flakey pastries. "You're in luck, we just baked some fresh."

"I'll take a coffee, too. Just black."

"Coming right up."

Margot watched as Casey's pink hairdo darted down the counter and to the coffee machine. The myriad smells had finally dissipated and the auditory background noise—or lack thereof—drew her attention. Most of the tables were empty and only a few patrons lined the seats by the front window.

"That will be six eighty," Casey said and set the mug and plate in front of Margot.

Margot dug into her wallet for a ten-dollar bill and slid her change into the tip jar. Casey's eyes widened.

"Thanks."

"I'm surprised it's not busier," Margot commented.

"We usually get a slow down around now.

Most of the kids are in school and folks are still at work."

"Isn't it school break this week?"

"You know, I think you're right. Guess it is a little strange."

Margot took her plate and mug, retreated to the nearest table. She expected Casey to go back to tending to any other customers who came in, but instead she stepped from behind the counter and pulled up a chair. "I hope it's okay if I sit. I was kind of hoping to talk to you about something."

"Sure. What can I do for you?" Margot sipped her coffee, savoring the bitter flavor.

"So, I graduated from high school last year, but I'm trying to save up to go to college."

"That's smart."

"Well, I was wondering if maybe you could help me apply to some seminaries." She tugged at her hair. "I know I'm not exactly what people would expect."

"Of course, I can help you. That's a wonderful path to choose. Have you picked out anywhere in particular?"

"Not yet. I was thinking out of state, though."

"Well, why don't you do a little research and we can touch base on what it involves."

Casey was out of her seat, throwing her arms around Margot's shoulders before Margot knew what hit her. "Thank you!"

Casey stepped back, ready to return to her post, when Margot held out a hand. "Can I ask you something?"

"Totally." Casey sat back down.

"Who makes all the teas and coffee that you sell?"

Casey cocked her head to one side. "Whoever is working. You just stick the tea leaves in and let it steep or the beans through the grinder."

Margot smiled, realizing her question

had been too vague. "What about the packages you sell as gifts?"

"Oh, that's usually Mrs. Henderson. Are you interested in any in particular?"

"Maybe. I'll let you know."

"Cool." Casey returned to the counter. Margot finished her coffee and croissants in silence, wondering if someone could have spiked Mr. Fayet's coffee with something. But she had no idea who, or with what.

5

Margot barely slept that night. Sam had gone radio silent, which didn't sit well with her. She had no doubt her cousin had learned something about Mr. Fayet's condition that would eventually prove useful. She'd spent the wee hours trying to come up with some explanation that might make sense and had hit a wall. *Am I just wallowing in my own failure?*

She presently paced her office, wearing a tread pattern into the carpet as she marched from the doorway to the desk and back again. On what must have been her twentieth pass, her phone rang on the desk. She expected Sam's face to be flashing on the screen, but it was an unfamiliar number. Given that it was five in the morning, not many people would be calling her.

"Hello?"

"Reverend, can I come over?" Amira sounded like she, too, had barely slept.

"Sure. I'll leave the front door unlocked."

Margot took the stairs two at a time after she grabbed a sweatshirt from her closet. She'd just turned the bolt for the front door when the outer knob turned and Amira appeared on the doorstep. Her hijab was askew and an early morning wind threatened to unseat it entirely. She must have already been on her way over when she'd called.

"Come in," Margot beckoned.

They settled in the living room on the couch. Amira studied her hands while Margot waited for the girl to open up.

"They said my father had antidepressants. That the medication might have caused the stroke."

"I'm so sorry to hear that. I know it's hard to learn that our parents aren't as perfect or healthy as we believe them to be when we are children."

Amira shook her head. "You don't understand. I looked everywhere. There weren't any pill bottles. My mother told the doctor they had to be wrong, because he didn't use medication."

There appeared to be a means behind Hassan's condition, but still no *who* and she didn't believe the proposed *why*. "Both of your parents will need you to be strong now as he recovers."

"If he recovers," she mumbled.

"Does your mother know you're not at home right now?"

"No."

"Don't you think she'd be worried if she

realized you were gone?"

Amira rubbed her eyes. "She keeps looking at me like I'm supposed to know what happened. Maybe she blames me, too."

"I refuse to believe that, Amira. Your mother loves you. Now, come on, I'm taking you home."

AMIRA WAS quiet on the trip across town. She looked more awake than when she'd appeared on Margot's doorstep, but she also seemed more sullen. Her father's condition clearly weighed on her. Margot hated that the girl blamed herself.

"You know my door is always open," Margot said, "but maybe try talking to your mother about what you're feeling. You shouldn't have to carry all of this by yourself."

Amira nodded mutely and climbed out of

the car. She was halfway up the driveway when Rebecca Davidson stepped onto her front porch, cup of tea in hand. She met Margot's gaze through the passenger side window of the car. Margot rolled down the window.

"Morning," Margot called and waved.

When Rebecca raised her hand to return the gesture, she stiffened. Rebecca's mouth seemed to be trying to form words, but her jaw tightened, prohibiting her from speaking. The cup shattered against the wood at her feet and Rebecca slumped against the railing.

6

In that moment, Margot detested seatbelts. It felt as though the belt were a living thing, clamping down on her torso to keep her immobile. Amira had already moved from her spot on the driveway. Finally, Margot freed herself from the belt and tumbled out of the car. She had her phone in hand, dialing 9-1-1 as she raced up the driveway.

"Support her head. Make sure she can still breathe," Margot told Amira as the emergency line operator came on.

"9-1-1, what is your emergency?" A pleasant male voice said.

"I need an ambulance to 1512 Cedar Road," Margot answered, only taking a moment to glance at the house number.

"Are you injured, ma'am?" The operator questioned.

"No. But a woman just collapsed. It may have been a stroke."

"Someone is en route to you now. Can you tell me if she's still breathing?"

Margot put the phone on speaker to free up her hands. She placed a hand above Rebecca's mouth to feel for breath, and watched Rebecca's chest rise and fall. "Yes, she's still breathing. It doesn't look like she suffered any other injuries from the fall."

"Look at her leg," Amira whispered, drawing Margot's focus.

Margot studied Rebecca's leg. Her pants were damp and as she slid the material up, she discovered angry red burns on the otherwise pale skin. "She may have suffered some slight burns from tea when she dropped the cup," Margot said.

"Okay. You're doing great. The ambulance is two minutes out."

Those two minutes stretched into eternity for Margot. She did her best to focus on keeping Amira calm and ensuring Rebecca was still breathing. She fought to keep her mind in the present and not back to that fateful day overseas that still haunted her dreams. When her unit had lost a brother-in-arms.

Just as the sirens wailed and the lights flashed at the end of the street, the front door opened and a bleary-eyed Moses appeared.

"Mom!" He fell to his knees at her side. "What happened?"

Margot didn't answer. Instead, she ended the call with the emergency line as the paramedics exited the ambulance.

"Step back," one of them said

Margot ushered both teens back to let the paramedics work. One of the medics looked at Moses. "This is your mom, right?"

Moses nodded.

The medic said, "Do you know if she has any medical conditions we should be aware of?"

"No. I don't think so." He squeezed his mother's hand and fought back tears. "Mom, please be okay."

Like the day before, Amira wrapped Moses in a tight embrace as the paramedics got his mother on oxygen and loaded her onto a gurney. Moses pulled free of Amira's arms. "I want to ride with her."

"Moses, why don't you let your dad know what's going on?" Margot suggested.

His normally mocha colored cheeks paled. "He's at work. I … I need to call him."

"The paramedics are going to take great care of your mom. I'll take you to the hospital after you let your dad know, okay?" Margot was beginning to feel déjà vu.

She watched the ambulance speed off toward the hospital and placed a hand on Moses's shoulder as he collected himself. Amira stepped up to his other side and took his hand in hers. "I'll go with you."

"Thanks."

"Remember our conversation about telling your mother where you were?" Margot prompted.

Amira glowered, but she let go of her friend's hand. All of the commotion had already drawn Mrs. Fayet from her house. She marched down the driveway in an overcoat, her hijab tucked neatly into the collar.

'What are you doing out here, Amira? What is going on?" She eyed Moses with clear suspicion. Her gaze narrowed and she pulled her daughter to her side in a rough gesture.

"Mrs. Davidson just had what we think

might be a stroke. We have to go to the hospital," Amira answered, yanking her arm free of her mother's grasp. "Besides, I want to see Daddy. He can't do morning prayers so someone has to do it for him."

Margot could tell Mrs. Fayet wanted to disagree with her daughter, but she said nothing. Instead she put a hand on her daughter's shoulder in a gentler motion. "We will get dressed and then we will go to the hospital to see your father."

Amira gave Moses one more quick hug and whispered something in his ear before following her mother into the house.

Margot ushered Moses to her car and pulled a U-turn in the middle of the street. She glanced at the boy beside her as he stared intently at his phone.

"Can you get ahold of your dad?"

"His work number went to voicemail and he doesn't usually have his cell phone on him while he's working. I'm going to try the main number."

Margot picked up on the hint of panic in the teen's voice and pressed her foot on the accelerator. She hoped it would convey a sense of urgency and that she took his fears seriously.

"Has your mom been feeling sick at all recently?" Margot finally asked when Moses hung up the phone having left a message for his father.

"She says she never gets sick. It's why she drinks all the tea she does. She says it's to keep her healthy. You know, I've never seen her get so much as a cold."

The more Margot learned, the more she was starting to believe that someone had targeted Mr. Fayet and Mrs. Davidson. But she still didn't know why or who. She highly doubted either Mr. Davidson or Mrs. Fayet had it in them to cause such a grievous injury to another person, even if their families were at odds. The only place she could see they had in common was the coffee shop. Again though, no one there would have any reason to harm either person that she knew of.

The hospital came into view, pulling Margot from her contemplations. She turned off the car and they walked into the Emergency Room side by side. Knowing that the doctors likely hadn't been able to discern anything yet, Margot led her young charge to the waiting area.

"Why don't I see if I can find you something to eat?" Margot told him.

"I'll keep trying to reach my dad."

"Good idea." Margot left him to make his calls. She had one of her own to make.

"Do you have any idea what time it is?" Sam grumbled when she answered Margot's call.

"It's not that early. I need you to get down to the hospital right now."

"What happened? Did Mr. Fayet wake up?"

"No. Mrs. Davidson had a stroke this morning on her front porch. At least it sure looked like one."

"What? Are you sure?"

"I saw it with my own eyes, Sam. I think something is definitely going on here, but I don't think it has to do with two families wanting to keep their kids apart."

"I'll be down there in ten."

"I'll see you in the waiting room."

Margot swung by the cafeteria and picked up a couple of muffins and some hot chocolate before returning to the waiting room. Moses sat curled up in one chair, staring out the window. His phone sat beside him on the arm of the chair.

"Any luck?" She asked as she set down the food.

"I left another message and texted him. I'm scared."

Margot settled into the seat beside him. "I know you are. But the doctors here are really smart. They're going to figure out what's going on."

"She and Dad didn't think I knew about all the police reports about the Fayets, but I did. It was such stupid stuff. Amira and I tried not to let it affect our friendship. It's kind of why we spent so much time at the church. It was a place we knew they wouldn't be at. At least not at the same time anyway."

"It must have been hard to have to choose your friend over your family."

"I didn't want to have to choose. I wanted both. I love my parents. And Amira is one of my best friends. Neither of us cared that the other practiced a different religion. It shouldn't matter, you know?"

"I don't disagree. Sometimes parents do what they think is best for their children, though. Still even they can be wrong."

"I'm going to have to call the college and rescind my acceptance." He sighed.

"I wouldn't do anything right now. You don't know anything about your mom's condition or recovery yet."

"Yeah, but people have problems after they have strokes. It messes with their brains. She's going to need me. Dad can't quit his job to take care of her."

Margot filed his concern away in her 'déjà vu' column. Something about the fact both Amira and Moses suddenly felt the need to stay close to home seemed more than a coincidence.

"Sorry to interrupt, but I need to speak to Margot," Sam said, tucking her sunglasses into the top button of her uniform shirt.

Moses's eyes widened at Sam's presence. "Why are the police here?"

"Sam's just here to talk to me. I didn't want to leave you until your dad came, so she came to me," Margot answered quickly before either of them had to explain that Mrs. Fayet had filed a police report about her husband's condition.

"Oh." He unfolded himself from the position he'd been in and scooped up one of the paper cups of cocoa and a muffin.

Margot led Sam into the hallway which was mercifully empty given the early hour. "I think someone has been targeting these people, but I don't think it's each other."

"What makes you say that?" Sam asked.

"Well, I mean, the Fayets and the Davidsons may have had petty issues with each other, but I refuse to believe they would inflict such physical damage on one another."

"So, who do you think is behind it?"

"I don't know," Margot said. "When you talk to the doctor, you should make sure they check to see if they find any antidepressants in Mrs. Davidson's system."

Sam's gaze narrowed. "How'd you know about that?"

"Amira confided in me this morning. She's having a really hard time dealing with all of this. When it first happened, she asked me if I thought it was Allah punishing her for wanting to go away to school."

"Mrs. Fayet insisted her husband didn't take antidepressants," Sam said.

"Yeah, Amira said the same thing."

"It's possible neither of them was aware of what was going on with him," Sam posited.

"It is, but I got the feeling he's the type of person who's too proud to accept the help that prescription medication would offer. If he had them in his system, I have a feeling someone else is responsible."

"But you think whoever is targeting them is using the pills to what, induce a stroke?"

"Maybe. Someone who knows about their feud. But I still don't see what the point would be," Margot answered and raked her fingers through her hair.

"Taking pills like that doesn't necessarily lead to stroke," Sam mused. "I mean, I'm sure there are other symptoms if you take too many."

"Did he have excessive levels in his system?"

"Pretty high, yeah."

"What if whoever did this didn't intend to cause a stroke?" Margot suggested.

"You think it was a mistake?" Sam didn't sound convinced.

"You'd have to take a lot of medication and I'm guessing they ground it up or crushed the pills. Otherwise he'd notice something off with his coffee. It would be pretty easy to not realize how much he'd been given."

Sam grimaced. "It wouldn't be the first time we'd seen someone use medication to induce symptoms."

"I was thinking the same thing," Margot said with a nod.

"But like you said, it seems less likely the Fayets and the Davidsons would target each other in the same way with the same result," Sam murmured.

"It has to be the coffee shop. Amira said she gives her father a couple pounds of coffee every year for his birthday and Rebecca got some bags of specialty tea for Chanukah."

"If someone was using those packages to deliver the pills unknowingly, wouldn't more people get sick?" Sam asked. "Wouldn't we have a rash of strokes?"

Margot shook her head. "Not necessarily. Each package is put together individually by Mrs. Henderson. But I have a feeling around the holidays, she probably has other people help out." *One in particular.* "And it's not that hard to grab a bag, stick in some coffee beans or tea leaves, and make it look like someone else did it."

"Your theory makes some sense," Sam

said, "but again, I'm pretty sure Mrs. Henderson isn't trying to cause severe neurological damage to her neighbors."

Margot wasn't sure that Mrs. Henderson was the one who'd packaged the gifts to Mr. Fayet and Mrs. Davidson. She didn't want to share her theory with Sam in case she was way off base. Besides, if her hunch turned out to be right, it was going to ruin a lot of lives.

7

Margot waited until Mr. Davidson finally arrived at the hospital—bleary-eyed and frazzled—to follow her hunch. Sam was busy getting the latest from Mr. Fayet's doctor as well as an update on Mrs. Davidson's condition. Margot stopped by Mr. Fayet's room in the ICU long enough to see mother and daughter kneeling in prayer on either side of his bed.

It was almost seven fifteen by the time

Margot made it to Henderson Coffee. For a shop that prided itself on early-morning beverages, they didn't actually open until seven thirty. She sat in her car in one of the few available spots on Main Street until she spotted an aproned worker through the front window. She didn't recognize the person, but she climbed out of the car and waited until they unlocked the door, flipping the sign to open.

"Can I get you something?" The teenage boy asked through a yawn. She'd half-expected Cameron to be working a shift.

"Just a coffee, black. I was also hoping to talk to Mrs. Henderson if she's around."

Her second request perked up the employee. He studied her in silence for a minute, ignoring the fact that she'd asked for a beverage. "Uh, I don't think she's here. Why? Is something wrong?"

"Oh, do you know if she'll be in later today?"

He shrugged one shoulder. "I don't know. Sorry."

"Thanks anyway." Margot waited while he retrieved her coffee in a to-go cup. At least he realized she wouldn't be sticking around.

After paying, she retreated to her car and sat there, sipping from the cup. It was just as good as the day before. She needed to talk to Mrs. Henderson to see if it was possible someone else could be packaging products for sale. Someone who wanted to hurt the Fayet and Davidson families. If Mrs. Henderson wasn't in, she'd have to go see if she was at home.

She made the familiar drive down to Cedar Road. She sped past the vacant homes of the Davidsons and the Fayets, pulling into the driveway of the Henderson family. She didn't see any movement from within, but that meant very little. The sirens had come and gone already. It was entirely possible they hadn't even paid attention to their neighbors' plight. If the in-fighting had been going on for years between the neighbors, it was possible the Hendersons and others on the street had either become accustomed to the drama, or had worked to tune it out.

She caught the flutter of a curtain corner in one of the upstairs windows as she strode up the front steps and rang the doorbell. The wait for the occupant to reach the first floor dragged on.

"Reverend Quade, is everything okay?" Sheryl Henderson, Cameron's mother, asked when she opened the front door in her slippers and a bathrobe.

"I was hoping I could come in and ask you a few questions. The other faith leaders and I are trying to figure out the best way to support the Fayets and Davidsons. Since you're their neighbor, I was hoping you'd be able to give us some insight."

"Of course. Please, come in."

Margot entered the Henderson home and took in the cherry wood paneling and the cream carpeting. "You have a lovely home."

"Thank you. Oh, what's happened to the Davidsons?"

Margot followed Sheryl into the kitchen with its granite countertops and collection of coffee makers. Apparently, Sheryl took her work home with her.

Margot took the seat offered before answering the question. "I'm not certain, but Rebecca collapsed this morning."

"Oh God. Do you know if she's all right?"

Margot shook her head. "No. It's strange, though, isn't it? What appears to be the same or at least a very similar illness striking two of your neighbors within days of each other?"

"I don't think that it's strange; it's heartbreaking for the families. I know after my

Daniel passed away; it was very hard to raise my children by myself. But I always relied on my neighbors. Honestly, I couldn't have gotten through it if it weren't for Rebecca and John, and Fatima and Hassan."

Mr. Henderson had passed away while Margot was at seminary and serving her tour of duty. She'd never met the man, but had heard only positive things from the congregation and people in town.

"I hope whatever is happening isn't a trend," Margot said.

"People don't spontaneously have strokes just because a couple people have them," she scoffed with the wave of her hand.

"Sheryl, I didn't say either of them had a stroke," Margot said. The tiny hairs on her neck bristled with nervous electricity.

"Maybe not Rebecca, but I heard from some of the nurses at the hospital that Hassan had a stroke," Sheryl answered coolly.

Normally, Margot wouldn't believe the hospital staff capable of such gossip. Still given the way the charge nurse had basically told Margot to solve the case, she didn't doubt the news of Hassan's condition was already circulating around town. The one downside of living in a small town, everyone knew everyone's business.

"You don't think someone could have targeted them, do you?" Sheryl blurted.

"I don't know. What makes you think that?"

Sheryl shook her head and studied her nails. "I don't mean to sound rude or anything, but I could understand one of them taking things too far with the other. They've been fighting over such petty things for years."

"None of it bothered you?" Margot prodded.

"What do you mean?"

"Well, from what I understand, the call to

prayer that started everything was very loud."

"I sleep with ear plugs in and a white noise machine. And if I'm honest, I sometimes take sleeping pills."

Could sleeping pills cause a stroke? "Did you know they both frequented your coffee shop?"

"I did. I have a standing coffee order for Hassan for his birthday and tea for Rebecca. I gave her a Chanukah gift this year, because she loves the lavender brew."

"You package everything yourself, right?"

"Yes. Why do you ask?"

Margot shook her head. "Nothing. It's a very kind gesture to provide for your neighbors."

"I know what you're doing, Reverend," Sheryl said.

"I'm afraid I don't know what you mean," Margot said, feigning ignorance.

"Something fishy is going on with Rebecca and Hassan. It's obvious you're trying to figure out why."

"I was in the right place at the right time I suppose. Besides, if I can offer support to people in need, I will."

Sheryl nodded. "Our kids look up to you. Of course you'd want to help them."

Margot's shoulder muscles relaxed. "I wouldn't want the kids to get hurt in all of this. How is Cameron holding up? It must be hard for him to watch his friends go through the trauma."

"He's been shut up in his room since the party actually. I can't get him to come out. I wish he'd talk to me."

"Maybe I could try?" Margot offered.

"If you think you can get through to him. I worry that with graduation coming and everyone else going off to college, it will trigger a relapse and Cam is going to spiral."

"Relapse of what?" Margot pressed.

"Depression," Sheryl answered, averting her gaze.

The bottom dropped out of Margot's stomach. The hunch was starting to solidify and she could even begin to see a reason why. "Please, I'd like to see if I can help. After all, I'm sure he would like to be the support his friends need."

Sheryl nodded. "His room is the second on the left when you get to the top of the stairs."

Margot took the stairs two at a time and reached the door. She knocked. "Cameron, it's Reverend Quade. Do you think I can come in?"

No response.

She knocked again. "I know it's early, but I was hoping I could check in with you. I wanted to see how you're doing."

Still no reply. Margot nudged the door inward with her toe, revealing a neat and orderly bedroom. The bed clearly hadn't been slept in the night before. That didn't bode well.

She chanced a quick look around the room to see if anything stood out to her. There was a small half-bathroom attached to the room and she spotted a pill bottle sitting on the sink. Margot grabbed a tissue, doubled it over and used it to spin the bottle so the label faced her. Cameron had a prescription for Zoloft. Based on the lack of pills—and the fact that the fill date was only a week ago—she had more than a hunch about what was going on.

She heard footsteps on the stairs below. She darted out of the bathroom back to the hallway, closing the bedroom door before Sheryl appeared on the landing.

"Is he being antisocial?" Sheryl asked.

"It's just early, and you know teenage boys," Margot said, shrugging. "They love their sleep. I'm sure I'll catch up with him later."

"I'll be sure to let him know you stopped by and wanted to talk to him," Sheryl said. "I just hope Moses and Amira reach out. Sometimes he isn't the best at letting people know he's around."

Margot gave a tight-lipped smile and started down the stairs. "How did Cam feel about how close Amira and Moses have become lately?"

"Close? Oh, you mean because they were dating."

"I didn't realize they were actually a couple," Margot answered.

"Not if their parents asked. But, to everyone else it was pretty obvious. Cam was actually the one who convinced Moses to make the first move and ask Amira out. He was thrilled they found each other."

"I'm glad." Margot made her way back to the first floor and the driveway.

She needed to get in touch with Sam and fill her cousin in on her suspicions. The last time she'd gone off on a case without police back-up, she'd had to face down a knife-wielding kidnapper. She wasn't in the mood for a repeat event.

8

The fact that Sam didn't answer set Margot's nerves on edge. She didn't want to leave the details in a message, so when voicemail picked up, she simply said, "It's Margot. I think I know what's going on. I'm headed to Henderson Coffee. I'd appreciate back-up."

She pulled into the same spot she'd vacated only a short time ago and marched through the front door. The same employee leaned on the counter, staring at his phone. The rest of the place was empty.

"Oh, hey again. Can I get you another cup of regular?" He asked, setting his phone aside.

"Actually, I'm looking for Cameron. Any chance he's in the back? Maybe helping with inventory?"

"Uh, nope. Haven't seen him." The boy's cheeks flushed and his gaze darted around the room, refusing to land on Margot.

That told her all she needed to know. "I really need to talk to him. His mother sent me and she's worried about him." She didn't like telling the young man a lie but desperation made her willing to blur the lines of truth if it meant saving a young man.

"He said his mom knew where he was," he said before realizing he'd given away something crucial.

"Well, he lied to one of you. Cam is going through a rough time right now and needs a friend. Do you think you could tell me where he is so I can help him?"

"Look, I don't know where he is. All he told me was he'd give me fifty bucks if I told anyone asking about him that he wasn't around and I hadn't seen him."

"Wait, you have seen him. When?" Margot needed to buy time until Sam arrived. She only hoped that it wasn't with sirens blaring and lights flashing. This kid was already worked up enough. He didn't need the added adrenaline rush of police busting through the door.

"He just said he was going somewhere he felt safe. Where everything made sense. I don't know what he meant by that. That's all I know." He bowed his head. "Am I in trouble?"

"No. You've been very helpful. Thanks."

Margot turned and left the shop just as Sam's police cruiser pulled up to the curb. With the engine still idling, Sam opened the passenger door from the inside of the car and Margot climbed in.

"Want to tell me what's going on?" Sam asked.

"I think I know who's behind this. We need to go to the parsonage," Margot answered.

"Why? And who's behind it? What did you find out, Margot?" Sam demanded as she pulled away from the curb.

"I think it was Cameron Henderson," Margot said, her heart starting to beat wildly in her chest. She took a slow breath to keep her nerves under control.

"Cameron? What makes you think that?"

"I did a little digging around and he's had a hard time since his father passed away. I always did get the feeling he wasn't planning to leave town after school. I wouldn't be surprised if he worried that he'd be abandoning his mother. So, he made the decision to stick around. He knew his friends were considering going off to school, and maybe he felt that same fear of abandonment."

"So, he poisons his friends' parents?"

"I know it sounds crazy."

"How long have you had the information?" Sam's tone came across as accusatory.

"I called you as soon as I figured it out," Margot answered, failing to keep annoyance out of her tone.

"It wouldn't be the first time you'd gone off without me after finding the big clue," Sam replied.

"You brought me into this, remember? You're the one who thought there was something suspicious about Hassan's condition."

"And I was right," Sam said, turning to face Margot from the driver seat.

"You're acting like I wanted this. I don't go looking for these cases. But it seems like every time they happen, I end up involved," Margot answered.

"Look ... I guess sometimes I feel like I can't do this without you beside me. It doesn't exactly look great for my career and sometimes I doubt myself."

Margot reached over and gave her cousin a pat on the arm. "You are a great police officer, Sam. Don't ever doubt that. Now come on, we have a kid to help." As Sam undid her seatbelt, Margot asked, "Did they find antidepressants in Rebecca's system?"

"They did. And they confirmed with both of their primary care doctors, neither of them were being prescribed anything like that."

"I'm guessing the antidepressant they found was Zoloft. That's the prescription Cameron had," Margot said and got out of the car.

"I'm still not clear on why he'd do this," Sam replied, following suit.

"Both Moses and Amira told me they're now thinking of putting their college plans on hold to stay and take care of their parents.

It would mean Cameron's world wouldn't have to change."

They rounded the back of the house and Margot tested the back door. She'd been sure to lock it the night before but it now sat ajar. She felt the rough marks left from someone picking the lock. She suspected Cameron was in crisis and needed someone to talk to.

"Let me talk to him alone. I might be able to convince him to come quietly."

"No. I'm going in with you, but I'll stay out of sight. He won't know I'm here," Sam said, clearly unwilling to let Margot walk into an unknown situation solo.

The back door swung inward on silent hinges and Margot entered the house. Given what waited inside, it felt eerie, like she wasn't supposed to be here. The feeling bothered her, because this was technically her home. Carpeting muffled their steps as they wound their way to the front of the house and the staircase down to the basement.

"Leave the door open," Sam whispered in Margot's ear.

Margot nodded her understanding and started down the stairs. A light was on already, which lent credence to her theory that Cameron waited below. She'd considered checking the church first, but given that the kids had worked to make this a safe space for themselves, it seemed the more reliable option. Besides, she couldn't be certain of Cameron's mental state, and checking a wrong location might cost her time.

"Cameron, it's Reverend Quade," Margot announced as she reached the bottom step.

"Are you alone?" He called.

"Is there a reason I shouldn't be?" She stepped into the light.

Cameron sat on the couch on the side that was set up like a den. His jacket lay beside him and Cameron looked like he'd spent most of the morning there. He had dark circles under his eyes and he was pale.

"Do you mind if I sit with you?" Margot gestured to the couch.

He moved his jacket, but didn't verbally answer her question. So, she sat beside him, hands clasped in front of her and resting on her knees.

"How are you doing, Cam?"

"Okay, I guess."

"I don't know that I agree with that statement. You don't look like you've slept in the last few days."

"I've just had a lot on my mind."

"You want to tell me what's got you staying up? I'd like to help if I can."

"You wouldn't understand." He wouldn't meet her gaze.

"You know, I might. I was a teenager once, believe it or not. I remember what it was like. A lot of stuff was confusing and it

wasn't anything I wanted to talk to my parents about."

"I don't want them to leave," he said.

"Them who?" She prompted, even though
she had an idea of who he meant.

"Amira and Moses. They're going off to
college in the fall and I'm not. I have to stay
and help Mom with the shop. She can't do it
by herself. Not since Dad died. I have to step
up and be the man."

"Did your mom tell you that you had to
stick around town?"

"Well, she didn't have to."

"So, you didn't talk to her about your
plans after graduation?"

"I thought it was obvious. It's what a good
son does. He takes care of his parents when
they need it."

"That's true. Can I ask, why you're sitting
down here alone?"

"Amira and Moses are busy."

"You don't think they'd appreciate having

their friend around to support them in their time of need?"

Cameron picked at his nails. "They wouldn't want to talk to me if they knew what happened."

"What did happen, Cam? Please, I want to help you, and I can't do that if you aren't honest with me."

"I did something bad."

"Bad things can be fixed," Margot said.

"Not this. What I did, it can't ever be taken back. I knew it was wrong when I was doing it. But I couldn't stop myself. It was like I wasn't in control of my body."

"What did you do, Cameron?"

"I just wanted to make them a little sick. So that Amira and Moses would stay here. So, we'd just keep hanging out, you know?"

"You made who sick?"

"Their parents. I just wanted my friends to stay, and I knew they would if they had to take care of their parents. It's what good kids do, no matter what religion you believe in."

"What you did was against the law. You know that, right?" Margot said, resisting the urge to pull the boy into an embrace. Despite what he'd done, he was still a child.

"I know. I've been down here trying to make peace with it. Mom's heart is going to break. Amira and Moses aren't ever going to talk to me again. I wish I could take it all back. I don't know how."

"By admitting what you've done to the people you've hurt. And taking responsibility for your actions, whatever the consequences may be."

"I'm scared."

"I know. But I can go with you if you want."

"I just wanted them to stay," he whispered and buried his face in his hands.

Footsteps on the stairs pulled Margot's

attention. Sam appeared at the bottom. "How's it going down here?"

Cameron's head shot up. "I thought you said you were alone."

"I was. Sam has a key," Margot said. It wasn't technically a lie. She'd come down alone and Sam did have a key in case of emergencies. To her cousin, she said, "Everything's fine. We're just talking through some things right now."

"I thought you would have been at the hospital," Sam said. Thankfully, she knew enough not to push Cameron before he was ready.

"We were just heading over," Margot said and stood up.

"Mind if I join you? I'm a sucker for the cafeteria bagels," Sam said with a smile.

"I don't see why not. Is that okay with you, Cam?" Margot eyed the boy as he, too, stood.

"Sure. I guess."

The three of them walked single file up the stairs and out to the front of the house where Sam's car waited.

"I walked back from the center of town," Margot said in the hope of allaying Cameron's suspicions.

"Oh."

Margot climbed into the back seat of the cruiser and patted the seat beside her. "Come on. It's okay."

He sat on the very edge of the seat with his knees pressed tight against the seat in front of him. He kept his hands planted firmly on his legs the whole ride to the hospital. When they pulled into a free space in the visitor lot, he tumbled out of the car, eager to get away. He wasn't ready to confess to the police yet, but maybe he would be ready to talk to his friends.

9

The ICU floor was quiet as they approached the first occupied room. Rebecca lay immobile in the bed, hooked up to monitors that tracked heart rate and respirations. A third monitor tracked what Margot had to believe were brain waves. Had her exposure levels been high enough to warrant inducing a coma, too?

"Cam!" Moses exclaimed, rushing to pull his friend into a hug. "I'm so glad you're here."

"I'm so sorry," Cameron said, pulling out of the other boy's grip. "I'm so sorry. It's all my fault."

"What are you talking about?" Moses looked from his mother to his friend and back again. "You didn't do anything."

Cameron shook his head. "Yes, I did. I was so scared of losing everyone … I'm going to anyway."

"You're not making sense," Moses said, shaking his head and taking a step back.

Tears streamed down Cameron's face as he looked at the floor. "It's all my fault. I made her sick. I knew she bought my mom's lavender tea all the time and so I started putting some crushed-up pills in her big orders."

Moses's jaw tightened and color flushed his cheeks as he put more distance between them. "No, you're lying."

Cameron tried to reach out a hand, seeking physical connection with his friend.

"I didn't think it would do this." He gestured to the motionless woman in the bed. "I thought it would just make her sick enough that you'd have to stay."

"Why would you do that?" Moses yelled.

"I was scared, man." Cameron's voice sounded thick, like he was holding back sobs. "I didn't want things to change. It was going so good with the three of us. Then you got accepted to an amazing school. And Amira was going to go off and do great things, too. I was just going to be here working in my mom's coffee shop for the rest of my life."

"She didn't ask you to do that," Amira's voice came from the hallway. She'd heard enough of the conversation that she side-stepped Cameron and moved to stand by Moses, her arm looped through his. "Did you make my dad sick, too?" She looked Cameron straight in the face.

"Yes," Cameron answered, his tone barely above a whisper. He wouldn't meet her gaze.

"He may never walk again, because of what you did."

He turned to look at Margot and Sam in the hallway. Margot was surprised the confrontation hadn't drawn more people. Cameron wiped the tears from his eyes and turned to leave the room.

He held his wrists out to Sam. "You can arrest me now. I'll write everything down. I'll plead guilty. Please just do it."

Sam's expression was grim, but she didn't pull out her handcuffs. Instead, she placed an arm around his shoulder and led him away from Amira and Moses as they clung to each other in stunned silence.

Margot was going to have a lot of work to do healing these wounds.

Six weeks had passed since Cameron's confession. Not surprisingly, the news had made it into the paper and everyone knew about what he'd done within a few days. Margot sat in her office at the church, preparing her sermon for the next morning, when a knock on the door interrupted her focus. She looked up to see Sheryl Henderson standing in her doorway.

"I'm sorry to drop by like this," Sheryl

said. "I was hoping you had a minute to talk?"

Margot waved the woman into the room. Sheryl pulled the door closed behind her and perched on the edge of the chair opposite Margot. She wrung her hands in her lap, twisting them until Margot heard a few joints crack.

"How can I help, Sheryl?"

"You know what they wrote about Cameron. The reporters called him un-hinged, but he's not. He was sick and he wasn't taking his medication." She leaned forward, resting her forehead on her hands. "God, it sounds like an excuse and that's not what I'm trying to do. I detest what he did. I didn't raise my child to hurt other people, but I didn't see how much he was hurting. Part of this is my fault for not seeing his struggle."

"You can't be there for your child all the time, no matter how much you wish it were the case. Besides I missed it, too," Margot said. "I spent a lot of time with him, Moses, and Amira. I should have seen something was off. When the others were animated about their prospects of moving away and starting a new chapter in their lives, I should have noticed the way Cam withdrew from the conversation and didn't engage."

Sheryl sniffled, and Margot moved around the desk to sit at the woman's side.

"I just don't understand why they would characterize him like that," Sheryl said. "I know he hurt people and I don't want to minimize what he did, but I just don't see how it helps anyone to say he was unhinged."

Margot clasped her hands together. "I don't agree with how the paper painted him either, because like you, that's not the boy I knew. Unhinged, that's not the boy that owned his misconduct either."

"I got a call from the lawyer today," Sheryl said. "They're not going to pursue a trial.

They're giving him a deal instead. He serves a year in a psychiatric facility, getting treatment, and then he'll be on probation until he's twenty-one."

"That sounds like a good deal."

"He keeps saying he wants to face what he's done. But I just want him to get help. How do I convince him to take the deal?"

"I don't think you can. But I might know some people who can. If it's okay with you, I'd like to see him."

"I think he'd appreciate a friendly face," Sheryl said with a nod. She dabbed at her eyes to keep the tears from falling. "Thank you for getting him to come forward."

Margot wrapped her arms around Sheryl as the other woman broke down. They sat in the office in silence as Sheryl let out her grief, anger, and whatever other emotions that needed to be expressed. Margot had been doing some of that herself. As a mentor, she'd failed Cameron and more importantly, she'd failed as a minister. Sure, she'd been able to convince him to open up and admit to what he'd done, but it shouldn't have come to that in the first place.

She would carry that sense of guilt for a long time to come, but perhaps there was a way to make the burden lighter. It would take some convincing, however she was hopeful her plan would work.

LOCK-UP IN PORT Marie wasn't what Margot had expected. Having never been there in her time being home from the Middle East, it surprised her at how clean and well-lit it was. Then again, the type of people who were held there tended to be less violent offenders. Cameron sat in the communal space, huddled in a corner despite the room being mostly empty.

"Hi, Cameron. Do you mind if I join you?" Margot asked.

He looked up at the sound of her voice and the edges of his lips tried to form a smile, but he resisted the urge. He returned his gaze to the wall. "I … I guess."

Margot settled against the hard-backed chair beside him. "How've you been feeling now that you're back on your medication?"

"Okay, I guess. Some days are better than others. How come you're here?"

"I wanted to check on you. I know this place can be scary. Didn't the judge let you go home to your mom?"

"He said I could leave, but I belong here."

"I don't think that's true, Cam. You aren't a bad person. You made a serious mistake, but you're working to fix it."

"You don't understand. They won't ever forgive me, so why should I get a chance to be back out in the world again? I deserve to be here."

"What you're feeling right now is guilt. It's a healthy emotion to feel after what happened. Punishing yourself like this isn't going to make things better moving forward." Margot looked around the space, trying to imagine Cameron spending years here. She pictured the toll it would take on his psyche if he were kept here when he would be better served elsewhere. "Your mother told me about the plea deal they offered you. She said you didn't want to take it."

"She told you?" He turned to face her, giving Margot his full attention. "I'm not worth it."

"Now, I know that's not true," Margot said.

"Why don't you hate me? I did the most un-Christian thing ever," Cameron said, his voice growing louder with anger bubbling just below the surface. "We're supposed to love our neighbors and I just ruined their lives."

"Because you aren't unlovable or unredeemable, Cameron. You are capable of being forgiven, but you won't be able to accept that forgiveness from others if you aren't able to first forgive yourself."

Cameron shook his head again. "I just don't think I can do that."

Margot reached out, about to place a reassuring hand on his shoulder when she caught herself. Simply telling him he needed to forgive himself wasn't going to convince him. Showing him that she understood his burden might though. "I'm not a doctor, but I know what it looks like when you have to carry a heavy burden. You keep it inside and don't let anyone in to help carry the load. It's hard and it's lonely, a place like this isn't going to do you any good."

"You saw stuff when you were in the military?" His tone conveyed a curiosity that he hadn't shone since he'd made his confession.

"I did," Margot said. "For a while I thought I had to bear that burden by myself. Eventually, I realized that it was better to talk about it with someone I trusted, who could understand how it made me feel. Being in a facility where you have access to programs that can help you learn to deal with your emotions isn't a bad thing. Still staying here, that's going to change your life in a big way … not for the better either. You have a chance to make amends."

"How am I supposed to do that? Amira and Moses won't even speak to me." The curiosity fled his expression and he huddled back into himself.

"That's not true," Moses' voice said from the doorway.

Margot and Cameron looked up. Both Moses and Amira stood there with visitor badges clipped to their shirts.

Amira held tight to her boyfriend's arm and it made Margot realize just how close the two of them had become. Margot wasn't expecting them to forgive Cameron all at once, but she'd been glad when they'd agreed to go with her to see him. He needed to know there was light at the end of this particular tunnel.

"You said you never wanted to see me again," Cameron whispered warily as Margot gave up her seat and let the other two teens join Cameron in the corner.

She remained nearby to observe the interaction. Both Moses and Amira had said they would come only if she was present. She wanted to oversee the three of them one last time.

"My mom is doing better. They think she'll have a little memory loss, but she will be okay otherwise," Moses said softly. "The burn on her leg has already healed."

"That's good," Cameron murmured.

"My dad came out of the coma three weeks ago," Amira said. "The doctor thinks he'll have some speech problems. He'll need to have physical therapy to help strengthen the left side of his body, but he's going to be able to walk again."

"Good," Cameron said again, not meeting either of their gazes.

"You should have said something to us. We could have talked about it," Moses said, his tone sharp.

"And said what?" Cameron asked, his voice miserable. "I wasn't going to convince you not to go away to school. I know I was being selfish wanting you to stay. I was scared of things changing. Anyways because of what I did, they have and no matter what happens, I can't make it go back to how it used to be. I don't deserve your friendship."

"I don't think we can ever go back to how it was before," Amira said. "We talked about it. We told our parents and the lawyers that we don't want you to go to jail. We want you to get help and get better. Show us that you can get better and maybe we can be friends again."

"She's telling the truth," Moses added. "If you want to start making it up to us, you'll take the deal. See the doctors and work out whatever is going on inside your head. That's where you start to earn us back."

Cameron chewed on his lower lip and looked over Amira's shoulder to Margot, as if asking her permission. He didn't need her approval to make this decision, but she knew he wanted someone in authority to tell him it was okay to begin healing. So, she nodded her head and smiled at him, conveying her approval without words.

"Okay. I'll do it. I'll take the deal," Cameron said.

Margot felt her own shoulders relax as Amira and Moses stood up. Moses offered Cameron his hand and after only a moment of hesitation, Cameron shook it. Amira released her grip on Moses' other arm and retreated to where Margot stood.

"I was really nervous coming here," she whispered.

"I know you were, but I know your father would be proud of you for extending an olive branch and starting everyone on a path to healing and moving forward."

"My father is going to need a lot of help for a while. I'm going to stay and defer college for a year. Just until he's back on his feet. Moses is still going off to school. It's what his mom wants him to do and I think, like me, he wants to make her as happy as he can right now."

"Please let me know if there's anything I can do to help your family," Margot said. "Your parents haven't always been interested in the charity of non-Muslims, but my door is always open to everyone, no matter their faith."

"Thank you. I don't know that they'll

change their mind, but at least I think the stupid feud will finally be over." Amira gave Margot a one-armed hug. "Thank you for being a friend."

"Of course. You are always welcome at my table and in my home. No matter what."

Moses joined them and they left Cameron to prepare for his future as Moses and Amira, too, prepared for theirs.

It wasn't always easy to love one's neighbor, especially in a world that tried everything to divide them. Margot had witnessed firsthand how people could come together irrespective of their religion to embrace one another as human beings. Even when the situation seemed grim, they were capable of seeing the good in others and giving them the chance to learn to love themselves again.

BROTHERS IN ARMS

Brothers In Arms

S.E. BIGLOW

 Created with Vellum

1

A brisk late-fall wind whipped down Main Street past Henderson Coffee. People milled about, clutching travel mugs and to-go cups tightly in their gloved fingers. It had been nearly two years since Margot had returned to Port Marie, and it was the very first time that she'd be marching in the Veteran's Day parade.

The parade had been a joint effort between worship leaders and the town council. Margot still couldn't believe how much support they'd received for the idea. Port Marie wasn't known for big displays, not even for Thanksgiving or the Fourth of July. This year though, they'd decided to honor the service of all the town's veterans. They even had someone from the Korean War marching.

Margot was standing on the front steps of the church studying the parade route. When footsteps echoed off the pavement in front of her, she looked up and broke out into a broad grin. Derek Nesbit stood at the bottom step with his wife, Catalina, by his side. Catalina carried a small child in a sling who gazed up at Margot with wide brown eyes and a mop of curly dark hair.

"I didn't think you were going to make it," Margot said, setting the paper aside and wrapping Derek in a tight embrace.

He smiled. "It's been long enough. Besides, I was born and raised in Port Marie. Why shouldn't I join the rest of you for this thing?"

"I'm really glad you came," Margot said

again before turning to Catalina and their daughter. "It's good to see you, too, Cat."

"And under much happier circumstances," the other woman replied.

Margot bent and waved at the girl. "And you must be Athena."

Athena giggled and grabbed for the dog tags and cross that hung around Margot's neck.

Margot beamed at her. "She's gotten so big. I remember when you sent me the birth announcement. She was such a little peanut then."

"She's going to be a 1 year old next month," Catalina said with a proud grin.

"Time is just flying." Margot's phone beeped in her pocket so she pulled it out to see a reminder she'd set for herself. Looking back up at the Nesbits, she said, "I hate to duck out, but we have to finalize the parade route so I've got to meet with the town council and the other faith leaders. I'll see you at the parade in the morning."

"Looking forward to it," Derek said.

Margot was glad to know that her old comrade had finally gotten the help he needed. After losing his uncle almost two years ago, he'd uprooted his family to escape the stigma Warren's death had brought out in the small town. He and his wife were happy elsewhere now, but he'd been comfortable enough to return for this one event. He even seemed to have dealt with the trauma that he and Margot had shared overseas.

She scooped up the proposed map route and headed for the parking area in front of Henderson Coffee where the group had agreed to meet. The location wasn't by accident. It had been an attempt on Margot's part to help the town heal from tragedy. Just eight months earlier Sheryl Henderson's son, Cameron, had poisoned his friends' parents.

Cameron was getting the help he needed and Margot knew that his actions shouldn't reflect on his mother. So, Margot had insisted that they have all of their planning meetings and even end the route of the parade at the coffee shop. She hoped it would help to encourage people to patronize the spot. Sheryl deserved to be a part of the community again.

Port Marie, like most small towns, had a long memory for the painful things that happened within its borders, and that wasn't always a good thing. Finding the truth wasn't always as healing as Margot wished it to be.

As Margot approached the spot, her cousin Sam pulled up beside her in her cruiser.

"Did I hear that Derek Nesbit is back in town?" Sam asked through the rolled-down window.

Margot was close enough to feel the heat blasting from inside the car. "He is. He's marching in the parade tomorrow. Is that a problem?"

Sam shook her head, her dark hair bouncing against her shoulders. "No, I was just surprised. I kind of thought he wanted nothing to do with the town."

"It's like they say, time heals wounds," Margot replied.

"Well I'm glad you have someone to march with tomorrow. I'm going to park and I'll meet you inside."

Given Margot's involvement in the planning, the Chief of Police had apparently decided Sam should be the person from the department liaising security. Not that Margot minded. Smiling to herself, she stepped into the warm confines of the coffee shop and spotted a familiar, pink-haired barista behind the counter.

"Hey, Casey," Margot greeted the young woman.

"Hi. Your usual?"

"Please." Margot fished money from her pocket while Casey prepared the coffee in a to-go cup. "Heard back on any of your applications yet?"

"Not yet. I really appreciate your help, though," Casey answered and passed her the coffee.

Margot settled herself at one of the tables overlooking the street. Someone—maybe Casey—had pushed a few tables together. Slowly, other people trickled in. Sam took up residence on Margot's right side and Laura Finch, the newest council member, sat on her left.

"I really hope folks turn out tomorrow," Laura said, sipping from a ceramic mug. In her thirties, she wore her dark hair in a thick braid down her back and her olive-green eyes tracked everyone else's movements with an intensity Margot usually only saw in her fellow soldiers. But to her knowledge, Laura had never served. She'd moved to town about eight months earlier and used her outside experience as her pitch for town council. She could bring new ideas to the town. Enough people had liked her ideas to appoint her. The parade was just the first of her plans to come to fruition.

"I think there's been enough buzz about it during services and around town that it's going to be well-attended," Margot said. Besides, she already knew of one reporter who'd been eager to provide coverage leading up to and after the event. Veronica Morris-Sawyer had spent much of her career as a small-town reporter digging into the cases of missing boys. When Margot and Sam had finally laid that particular mystery to rest, she'd turned her attention to reporting on more positive things in town. So, Veronica had leapt at the chance to cover the parade.

"Are you sure we even really need this meeting?" Laura asked. "I don't mean to sound ungrateful or anything, but we already talked about the route at the last meeting. Why can't we just go along with that plan?" Her tone implied she had other things she'd rather be doing. However up until this point, Laura had insisted on having more meetings than strictly necessary to make sure every single aspect of the parade was nailed down.

That's odd. I wonder what is pulling her attention? Margot set down her cup and turned to the woman on her left. She opened her mouth to answer, but Sam jumped in before she could say a word.

"There wasn't a police presence at your last meeting. Chief Yawkey just wants to make sure we have enough people to maintain security."

"Are you expecting something to go horribly wrong?" Laura asked with a high-pitched laugh.

"No, but we need to be prepared just in case something does happen. Knowing where people are supposed to be makes it obvious when folks are where they shouldn't be. We don't want some kid who thinks he's a genius defaming property."

"Oh … right, of course," Laura said with a hint of sarcasm. "I should have realized that."

The rest of the group finally arrived and they spread the route Margot had drawn out across the table. The parade would start by the high school track and wind its way through the town, following the curve of Main Street past the church, then finally to end down at the coffee shop. Sam passed around a listing of traffic cameras that overlapped the route.

"I don't like this blind spot here," Sam said, pointing to a stretch of Main Street that lacked coverage right before the end of the route.

"But we have coverage leading up to it and right after it. It's maybe going to be out of sight of cameras for five minutes as everyone moves through. Less if people are marching fast," Laura urged.

Sam made a note to herself on her copy of the route that Margot could see read 'double officers' with an arrow pointing to the spot. Margot appreciated Sam wanting to keep both the participants and onlookers safe, but she had to agree with Laura. While their small town had experienced its share of tragedies, there'd never been anything like an attack during a large event. This town overall was a safe place. Still if having extra officers on scene made Sam more comfortable, she wasn't going to protest.

THE NEXT MORNING DAWNED COLD, but with clear skies. Margot stood in the bathroom straightening her uniform tie. Her hair, which had grown longer since she'd returned home, was slicked back in a tight bun at the nape of her neck. The cross and dog tags she always wore hung visibly against her chest.

"Knock, knock," Sam said from the doorway.

Margot turned to find her cousin in her own dress blues. "You look good."

Sam smirked. "You, too. I figured I could get dressed up for the occasion."

"Well, not that you need mine or anyone's approval, but I highly approve."

They made their way down to the first floor and donned jackets before stepping into the cold November air. Given that they'd be using the main roads in town for the parade route, Margot and Sam traveled on foot to the back of the high school. Margot hadn't set foot on the campus in over a decade. No doubt it would look much smaller than what she remembered from her time there.

"I'll let you get lined up. I want to run

through logistics with my people one more time," Sam said and headed off in the opposite direction.

Margot stopped at the edge of the track that encompassed the school's football field. She remembered running laps there after she'd graduated, conditioning her body to be Army ready before she even hit basic training. This place had shaped her more than she realized.

"Bring back memories?" Derek asked, appearing at her side with his cap tucked under one arm.

"It does. Good ones, believe it or not."

"A lot happened in this place, didn't it?" He sighed.

Margot made a noise of agreement and tugged on the hems of her gloves, wishing they were longer. "You clean up well, Private."

"You, too, Chaplain. So, is it just us

marching together, or are we joining someone else?"

"The parade is organized by military branch. We figured since there isn't a ton of veterans from any one unit, that was easier. Besides, we liked the idea of seeing those that served across the generations marching together."

"I like it."

"Where are Cat and Athena?" Margot asked.

"Cat said she'd be waiting at the end of the route for me."

"Well, I look forward to seeing them again."

"Anyone in the onlookers for you?"

"My parents said they'd try to come," Margot said. "And Sam is working the police detail."

Derek's smile faltered at the mention of Margot's parents.

Gently, Margot asked, "How are you holding up being back, Derek? Really?"

He cleared his throat. "We went to see Aunt Mary. She's doing okay. However, it was the first time we'd seen her in nearly two years. She looks different. Her hair is shorter and she's so pale. Looks almost like she never goes outside anymore."

"And what about Rosalinda? Have you visited her?"

Derek let out a harsh bark of laughter. "We actually visit her twice a month. I know they're both responsible for Uncle Warren's death, but somehow, I blame her less than Aunt Mary. Maybe it's because he was so horrible to her at the end? I feel guilty some-times about treating them differently."

"You have every right to feel the way you do. Remember, healing takes time and it takes many forms. You are making great strides in finding a way to be in their lives again. It isn't going to happen overnight." Margot caught sight of the local Rabbi circling the troops. "Come on, it's time to line up."

They got into formation behind the two soldiers carrying a banner with the Army crest and motto. Their group was the largest of the branches, followed by the Navy, then the Marines, and the Air Force. Being around so many people in uniform brought Margot right back to her time overseas. They weren't in tactical gear now, but they might as well have been. Her attention to detail heightened and she counted the number of people in her makeshift unit: fifteen. *We'll all get to the end together.*

The parade moved out, led by the high school marching band and flag corps. Margot's pace fell in step with those around her and the beat from the drummers in the band. As soon as they left the nestled space of the high school, loud cheers swelled all around them. People lined the streets and waved flags. Every notice about the event had expressly prohibited throwing items at the marchers, even things like candy.

As they slowly made their way toward and around the church, Margot spotted uniformed police immersed in the crowds. It appeared everyone in town had come out to show their support. Just as they reached the front of the church, Margot broke out into another broad grin as she spotted Mr. and Mrs. Fayet sitting beside Mr. and Mrs. Davidson. Amira sat between them, holding up a tablet with Moses' face on it. He'd been home for fall break already and had been sad to miss the parade.

"Hey Margot!" His voice called from the tablet as she slowed her pace.

"I love this," Margot shouted, giving the two families a thumbs up. She hadn't expected the neighbors to resolve their differences so quickly, but maybe suffering similar setbacks had helped them bond. Maybe there was a little good that had come out of what Cameron had done.

"Thank you for your service," Amira called as Margot felt a hand on her back, ushering her onward.

"Friends of yours?" Derek said in her ear.

"Yes. I'll tell you all about it later."

Derek returned to his spot on the far end of the group. They rounded the church and started on the final leg of the march up Main Street to the end of the route. The band was still playing up ahead, but she couldn't hear it as clearly. But, like the good soldiers they were, her group stayed in perfect unison as they marched onward. Despite knowing the route and the extra security Sam had put in place, Margot couldn't help feeling a sense of unease settle over her as they came up on the small stretch of road that didn't have traffic cameras.

Margot instinctively searched the crowds for signs of blue-uniformed officers. She caught sight of Sam in the crowd for a brief moment, but then she was gone. Margot's lungs burned as she held her breath until they were through the spot. Her chest ached as she exhaled, but she continued to march on, the band's music swelling now that they were closer to the musicians. As each section of the parade reached the end of the route, they moved off to the park that sat opposite the coffee shop. Families gathered to shake the hands of veterans they knew, all bundled in hats, coats, and gloves.

She stepped off to the side and watched as the Air Force brought up the rear of the parade. As Margot scanned the crowds for familiar faces, the tantalizing scent of barbeque filled her nostrils. She gravitated to the area that had been set up for food. She accepted a plate of ribs and pulled pork before going in search of Sam to debrief. She made it halfway back to the gathering spot when Catalina raced toward her, baby

Athena bouncing against her mother's chest in the carrier.

"Have you seen Derek?" Cat asked, breathless.

Margot shook her head. "I'm sure he's around here somewhere. The Army contingent was gathering just up there." She pointed to a spot filled with uniformed men and women milling about.

"I looked and he's not there. I checked the food area, too. I didn't see him when you all were coming to the end of the route."

"That doesn't make sense. I know he was at the other end of the group but I swear I saw him come through with us." *Or did he?* "There are a lot of people here, I'm sure he's just catching up with old friends," Margot added, resolving to find Sam and double check that everything went as it was supposed to. "If I see him, I'll let him know you're looking for him."

Margot took off in the direction she'd

seen some of the police gathering. She stepped up to the collective and spotted the chief of police among them. It wasn't difficult to spot the man as he stood at least a good six inches above the rest of the officers around him. His caramel-colored skin looked pale and his brown eyes darted over the civilians. Odd behavior considering he'd given Sam the directive to be the point person both on the committee organizing the parade and on the day.

"Chief, have you seen Officer Raymond?" Margot called.

He turned to look at her and his face fell. "Reverend Quade ... We have a situation. Officer Raymond has been taken."

2

The chief's words seemed to take ages to process in Margot's brain. The world around her went hazy and her hearing dulled. Black spots popped in her vision as the weight of what he'd said hit her.

"What … What do you mean she's been taken? I saw her on the parade route. She was manning the one place that didn't have traffic camera coverage."

"She was there, Rev. However, by the time the last group from the parade made it through, she was gone and she isn't responding to her radio either."

"Are you sure she's missing and not just off dealing with another matter?" Margot's throat felt raw as the words left her. She knew as well as they did that Sam would never leave her post without a good reason.

"Literally everyone in town is here," Chief Yawkey answered in a grim voice. "We've checked and she hasn't shown up on any of the other feeds after the blind spot either."

Dread danced down Margot's spine, cold and nauseating. Sam had been worried something could happen in that small stretch of a blind spot. Sadly, she'd been right. The food on the plate in Margot's hand suddenly turned unappealing and she tossed it into a nearby trash can.

"Did you see anything suspicious before or after you last had contact with her?" the chief asked.

Margot shook her head, struggling to

concentrate. She forced herself to remain present and in the moment. If something had indeed happened to her cousin, Sam would need Margot to be clear-headed and focused.

"Margot!" Catalina yelled, racing toward them fast enough that Margot worried for the baby's safety. Catalina thrust her phone at Margot. "I just got this."

Margot took the phone and looked at the image on the screen. The background was nondescript and dark. It could have been anywhere in town or somewhere beyond Port Marie's borders. It was clearly taken today, because Derek was in his uniform. He sported a bloody lip and the beginnings of a black eye.

"There's a message," Catalina rasped.

Before Margot could get to the message, her phone vibrated in her pocket with an incoming text message. An unknown number had sent her two texts.

She had a feeling she knew what waited

beyond the lock screen of the phone. *Please Lord, let Sam be okay.*

Her mouth went dry as she opened the message app. A photo like the one of Derek appeared on her screen. Sam had a bruise already visible on her cheek and a gag in her mouth. Margot's hands shook as she scrolled past the image to the message below it.

Will you save her in time?

"Let me see the message on yours," Margot said, turning her attention to Catalina's phone. A quick look told her the message to Catalina wasn't meant for his wife. It read: *Will she save him this time?*

"Two different messages, but it looks like whoever took them has both of them in the same location," Margot said. She could do this, use her logic and focus. Somehow, she would have to push down the panic. Sam and Derek needed the disciplined soldier in her.

"It's probably best that you two come back to the station and give statements," the chief said.

"But we don't know anything. Can't you track their phones or something?" Catalina asked, her entire body shaking.

"Whoever took them likely used their phones to get our numbers and then turned them off. Maybe even took the battery out and tossed them afterward," Margot answered robotically.

"How do you know that?" Catalina asked.

"Because, unfortunately, with the wealth of information available on the internet, it's easy to find out what to do to avoid police detection." Margot murmured, fighting back the rising tide of panic threatening to wash over her again. "We should go down and give our statements."

The chief left a few uniforms to corral the public and keep things orderly at the parade site as he, Margot, and Catalina walked back to the station. The station was eerily empty and quiet, with everyone otherwise occupied. Margot passed Sam's desk and stopped, almost like muscle memory from all the times before when she'd been required to give a statement.

"Mrs. Nesbit, why don't I take you first? So, you can tend to your daughter." the chief suggested.

Catalina had gone quiet on the walk over. She nodded mutely, her arms wrapped protectively around the child who was now slumbering in the carrier, her head pressed against her mother's chest. Catalina stepped into the chief's office and he closed the door, leaving Margot alone in the bullpen with her thoughts.

Her gut told her that this was not a coincidence. Someone had to know about the blind spot in the route and had clearly taken advantage of it. Although Sam had made sure to have an extra police presence there. *But I didn't see extra police when I went by.* Whoever had taken Sam and Derek also hadn't had a very large window of time to do it in. A lot of planning and forethought would have had to go into the kidnapping.

Margot sat at one of the desks and studied her phone again. The messages had to be different for a reason. Had Sam seen something go wrong with Derek and tried to intervene? Was she just collateral damage? If that was the case, who would want to target Derek? Other than what had transpired with his uncle, Derek didn't have any enemies in town. At least, none that Margot knew about.

She had to assume that whoever had taken Sam and Derek had a timeline for whatever plan they were following. If she had to guess, the timeline wasn't very long either. Margot needed to act quickly, but she also knew it would do her no favors to run off without giving her statement to the police. So, she found a blank piece of paper and a pen and drafted her statement, leaving a sticky note on it for the chief explaining that she'd be back to formalize and sign it. She had people to bring home.

3

The news of Derek and Sam's disappearance hadn't yet hit the town gossip mill, a fact for which Margot was extremely grateful. She saw officers circulating among the crowd, but they hadn't let the fear from one of their own having gone missing impact how they presented themselves.

"You were right," Laura Finch said from the crowd as Margot approached the food area.

"Sorry?" Margot turned to look at the woman.

"Oh, just that folks did turn up. I had my doubts, remember? But you knew they'd come and it turned out to be a great event."

"Thanks. You know, I'm actually a little busy at the moment. Do you know where the rest of the committee is?"

Laura's brow furrowed. "No. Is there a problem?"

"There's been a breach in security and the police have asked that I check with the committee to be sure no one inadvertently leaked anything they shouldn't have."

"Security breach? Wait, I thought that's why we had the police working with us?"

"Please, can you just point me to where everyone is?" *I don't have time for this.*

Laura huffed in apparent irritation. "I think they were all meeting by the food tents."

They started to wind their way through

chatting families with children chasing one another around and through the stalls that had been set up.

"When you said 'inadvertently leaked' information, what do you mean exactly?" Laura pressed as the rest of the committee came into view.

"Anything that we weren't supposed to be sharing with the public," Margot answered.

Laura looked down at her hands. "I mean, I told folks we wanted people along the whole parade route cheering the vets on. So, I made sure people were everywhere. You mean like that?"

Margot stopped walking and inhaled cold air, letting it shock her lungs. She hoped it would give her a momentary distraction from the mixture of panic from Sam and Derek's situation and irritation at Laura's seemingly ignorant statement. "No, that's fine."

She gave a nervous hiccup of laughter.

"Okay, good. I thought I was in trouble for a minute."

Margot resumed her trek across the food area to the rest of thc committee who sat gathered around a picnic table. A few gave Margot a friendly wave as she approached. *Lord, give me strength to deliver this news.*

Clearing her throat and holding her hands tightly behind her back to hide their trembling, Margot said, "We've had a security breach. The police have asked me to check with the committee to make sure no one gave out details of the parade route ahead of time."

Everyone shook their heads.

Reverend Hawley, who'd been sitting at the far end of the group, stood up and rounded the table. He moved slower than she remembered, a sign of her mentor's advancing age. "I didn't, but can I ask you a question in private?"

Margot left the group as they fell into

muted whispers. No doubt they were wondering what exactly the security breach entailed and why Margo had been sent instead of Sam to investigate the situation.

"You're not saying something. Please, I'd like to help," Reverend Hawley whispered. He'd been able to help her, however unwittingly, with the Conrad Baptiste case. Besides Margot's usual partner in crime-solving, Sam, was now the one in need of rescue.

"Derek Nesbit and Sam have been taken …" Her voice caught. "Kidnapped. Likely from the small area that didn't have video surveillance. That's all we know so far."

"Taken?" Reverend Hawley asked, surprise making his voice rise in pitch. "You're sure?"

Margot passed him her phone with the image of Sam and the threatening message still visible.

He shook his head and put a hand on

her shoulder. "Oh, Margot, I'm sorry. Do you know why they would have been targeted?"

Shaking her head, she answered, "Not that I can think of. I'm supposed to be giving the police my statement, but I can't shake the feeling that this is somehow personal. Also, our window to find them is going to shrink quickly."

"Anything I can do to help, I will. Just name it."

Margot eyed the group of faith leaders and council members. "You know most of the people on the committee personally. You don't think any of them would have shared the one weakness in security with anyone, do you?"

Reverend Hawley followed Margot's gaze. "No. They are all good people. I know that we've had some tragedies in the past. It has even felt as though people we thought we knew had done horrible things, but I don't believe anyone in this group would do that."

Margot took her phone back, studying the image of her cousin in as close detail as she could. Aside from the obvious injuries from being punched or struck in the face, Sam's head drooped to one side like she was groggy. Obviously a blow to the head could incapacitate someone and make them disoriented, but Sam looked almost asleep. Margot needed to compare it to the image of Derek, which meant a return trip to the police station. First though, she had one more group to speak with.

THE ARMY CONTINGENT sat huddled under the one tree with any leaves left on it. Most had set their hats aside and had taken jackets brought by family members. Everyone still had their gloves on. Margot tried to recall the marching formation. Knowing who had been in front, behind, and beside Derek would narrow her questioning. The faster she could return to the station with any additional information the better.

"Where'd you run off to, Chaplain?" Sergeant Don Veno asked. Sergeant Veno had served during Desert Storm and his salt and pepper buzz cut had gone even more salty in recent years. His time out of active service had been good to him. He'd married and settled down in Port Marie. He and his wife Serena had two young children.

"Sergeant, you were marching near Private Nesbit, weren't you?" Margot answered his question with one of her own.

"He was behind me for most of the route. He stepped out of formation around the church, though."

"Yeah, I know. He was asking me something, but I saw him return to his spot before we rounded the back of the church. Did you notice where he went?"

"No, sorry."

"You asking about Derek?" Thomas Rosen, a lieutenant, asked, interrupting the conversation.

"I am. You didn't happen see where he went, did you? I've been trying to find him, but he wasn't with us when we reached the end of the route."

"Yeah, I saw him. He was next to me until right before the end," Lieutenant Rosen answered.

"Where'd he go?" Margot tried to keep the rising panic out of her tone. She needed to remember that she had training. It didn't matter if she was tracking down a missing child or chasing a killer. She needed to approach the situation methodically.

"Just as we were coming up on the final turn, he stopped, pointed at someone in the crowd, said something, and took off running into the crowd."

"Could you tell what he said?"

"He mumbled it under his breath and took off so fast I didn't really hear. Something with a P, I think. Like Peter."

That icy chill of dread washed over Margot again. "You're sure he said Peter?"

"Like I said, he mumbled it under his breath. But that's what it sounded like."

Margot swallowed the lump in her throat. "Thank you."

She took off at a flat-out sprint back to the police station. Apparently not all of the ghosts from her past were dead and buried.

4

That icy feeling of dread that had overtaken Margot when she'd first seen the pictures of Sam and Derek returned as she skidded to a halt outside the police station. *He couldn't have seen Peter.* Peter had been dead for over two years.

"You can't just take off like that," the chief chastised her when she walked back through the front door.

"I'm sorry, Chief, but I have some more information. One of the other Army veterans saw Derek take off in the blind spot."

"So, he wasn't abducted?" Catalina asked, rocking Athena in her arms.

"I don't know. The other officer said he thought he had heard Derek say 'Peter' before taking off."

"By the fact you look like you've seen a ghost, I'm guessing he couldn't have seen Peter," the chief commented.

"Private Peter Abrams was killed in action during our tour of duty two years ago. It's a situation that both Derek and I struggle with."

"Derek had said a good friend of his was killed during his tour. He blamed himself," Catalina said.

At least Derek had finally shared some of the details with his wife. When Margot had reunited with Derek upon her return to civilian life, he'd been holding onto that trauma tightly, not willing to let anyone share the burden. Margot believed she'd moved past the loss, but it seemed that Derek hadn't.

"Derek was supposed to be driving the day we struck an IED. Instead, Peter was assigned as the driver and took the brunt of the damage. He died in our arms," Margot said, wiping tears out of her eyes.

"My God," Catalina breathed.

"Peter Abrams doesn't sound familiar," the chief said, rubbing his chin.

"Peter didn't grow up in Port Marie. He was from Maine. He said he was the first person in his family to enlist," Margot replied.

"Well, this is useful information, Reverend. Now, I want you to finish your statement. Then the both of you go home and wait. Let us handle things," the chief ordered.

"Understood," Margot replied.

"Is it okay if I wait for you to finish? I don't want to be alone right now." Catalina eyed Margot with a hopeful expression.

"Of course, you can."

Margot followed the chief into his office, reread what she'd written down as her statement, and added the new information she'd gleaned from talking to her fellow soldiers. "I spoke briefly with the rest of the planning committee and no one said they shared the details about the blind spot with members of the public. Although, if someone was standing in the crowd and Derek saw them, that makes more sense."

"Still that doesn't explain why Officer Raymond vanished, too," the chief muttered.

"Maybe she saw Derek step out of formation and went to investigate," she offered, more to convince herself than the man across the desk.

"Sounds like Officer Raymond to me." He glanced away from her for a moment and then added, "I admire your calmness, Reverend. I really do."

"If I'm not strong for them, I'm afraid I'd fall apart."

He passed her the printed, finalized version of her statement and she scribbled her signature at the bottom.

She said, "If you hear anything else, please let me know."

"If you or Mrs. Nesbit get any more messages from the kidnappers, you let us know, too. Don't go off investigating on this one by yourself, Reverend."

"Solving crimes isn't in my job description, Chief." Margot gave him a sad smile before joining Catalina in the bullpen. "We can go back to the parsonage and wait for news."

Catalina shook her head. "Actually, if you don't mind, I'd like to go to the church. To pray."

Margot should have known how much she needed to pray on the situation. It didn't really hit her until she and Catalina stepped through the narthex and into the sanctuary. Everyone was still down at the parade ground, enjoying each other's company, so the church was empty.

"I can pray with you," Margot offered.

"I'd like that."

The two women sat side by side and bowed their heads. Margot felt the weight of the chain around her neck, as if the memory of her service tried to weigh on her. She had nothing to feel guilty about with regard to Peter's death and neither did Derek. It was a last-minute change of assignment and the IED had been a hazard of the job overseas.

"Aren't we supposed to say something?" Catalina whispered.

"God knows what is in our hearts. We don't need words, unless that's how you usually express your faith. For me, it's more about being in the stillness and knowing God is there."

"Do you think God is watching over Derek and Sam right now?"

Margot gave Catalina's hand a firm squeeze. "I know it."

They sat in the calm stillness of the space with Athena still asleep in the carrier. Margot focused on her breathing, keeping it slow and even. With her free hand she wrapped her fingers around the cross hanging from her neck and sent up a silent plea. *Show me the way to bring home those I care about. Let them be safe from harm.*

"Do you really think Derek saw Peter?" Catalina interrupted Margot's prayer.

"I don't know. Sometimes soldiers are reminded of what they've seen by a glimpse of a face or a smell. War wreaks havoc on a person's sense of memory though."

"I thought we were in a good place. He's

been going to therapy twice a week. He's even in a veteran's group."

"Just because he thought he saw a dead friend doesn't mean the steps he's been taking to deal with the trauma aren't working. Honestly, Veteran's Day can be a rough time for a lot of people who've served."

"I just hate that he's out there, someone has him, and he's in danger. I thought I could stop worrying about that when he came home."

"We're all going to get through this." Margot needed to believe in her own words as much as Catalina.

"Why do you think the message was different?" Catalina blurted.

"I don't know. Do you still have yours on your phone?"

Catalina retrieved her phone from a pocket on the baby carrier. "The chief took copies already."

Margot studied the image of Derek. He

looked more alert despite the fat lip and possible black eye. Which meant Derek had probably been the target and Sam was just collateral damage. She scrolled down to look at the message from the kidnapper. The fact that the message said "this time" meant whoever had taken Derek assumed she hadn't saved someone "last time." Although, Margot couldn't be sure she was the "she" the message referenced.

"What is it?" Catalina asked as the baby stirred, giving a yawn and sleepy gurgle.

"It's just that the message to you is odd. Whoever is behind the kidnapping had to know that you and I knew each other, and that I knew about Peter."

"And that I'd show you the message," Catalina added.

"Exactly." Although, if they both received messages, it was possible that they would have seen the other in dealings with the police. Margot tried to run through the people who would have had knowledge of Peter's death and the specific circumstances behind it. Their unit had been small. As far as Margot knew, two of the other soldiers had re-deployed recently so they wouldn't be around. That left only one other person.

"What was he like? Peter, I mean." Catalina interrupted Margot's mental inventory.

"He was a young kid. The youngest in our unit by far, but he was a sweet guy. He loved to tell jokes and make everyone else smile. His death hit us hard. Obviously, Derek took it the hardest."

"I don't know if you can tell me, but why wasn't Derek the one driving? Not that I'm ungrateful that my husband made it home to marry me, but was there a reason?"

"You know, I don't remember the circumstances about that. It's funny what you do and don't remember."

They fell into silence as Margot returned

her attention to anyone who would have known about Peter's death. Of the other members of the unit who were back from their time overseas, there was only one other person, their commanding officer, Jackson Flannery. Although last she had heard he was stationed on a military base in Georgia. Still, it was worth a call to check he was where he'd said he was going to be.

"Would you excuse me? I need to make a call." Margot stepped past Catalina out of the pew and headed for her office.

She closed the door to the office and pressed her back against the cool frosted glass that took up the top half of the door. It was enough to shock her system into refocusing her attention. Derek and Sam needed her. She darted around the desk to the computer and pulled up her contact list to find Jackson's personal number. He might not answer, but it was a place to start.

The line rang five times and Margot was

about to hang up when a familiar gruff, bass voice answered. "Who is this?"

"Jackson, it's Margot Quade," Margot said.

"Aren't you a ghost from the past," Jackson said, a hint of surprise in his tone.

"Funny you should say that." Margot started to pace behind the desk, as far as the phone cord allowed. "I was hoping you had a minute to talk."

"I have a minute, sure. For you, heck, I've got two," Jackson said, and Margot could hear the smile in his tone. For an Army commander, he was a happier guy than most would believe.

"Derek Nesbit's been abducted," Margot said, "and I think it has something to do with Peter Abrams' death two years ago. I was hoping you might know what happened to the rest of the guys in our unit?"

"Damn. Forgive the language, Chaplain."

"Given the circumstance, I think a little

profanity may be in order." Margot paced back the other direction.

"Well, you two went back to where was it … Vermont?"

"Yes, Sir."

"Then another two of our boys re-enlisted and are overseas. And that just leaves Private Parnell. I think he stayed Stateside."

William Parnell hadn't been close to Peter—not like the rest of the unit. Margot often thought William had been a bit jealous of the easy camaraderie Peter enjoyed with the other soldiers and even with some of the locals. William had been a bit of a loner. He'd come from the Midwest. New Mexico, if Margot recalled correctly. He'd been back at base the day Peter died. He'd had no involvement whatsoever.

"He's back in New Mexico, isn't he?" Margot prompted.

"Believe so."

That did little to point to a potential culprit. William had no real reason to hold things against either Margot or Derek. Also, she didn't think he was the type of person to harm innocents either.

She said, "One last question, Sir."

"Sure."

"Do you know who notified Peter's family about his death?"

"Not personally, no. It's probably in his file though."

In that case she had no way of accessing it. Sam could have found a way to retrieve the information if they'd been able to work together, but Margot was going solo on this case.

"Thank you," she said.

Jackson said, "You think this had to do with Peter?"

"Yes. According to reports, Derek said Peter's name before he went MIA. Sir, you should also know that it appears my younger cousin, who is a police officer, was taken as collateral. Anything you can do to help would be much appreciated."

"Is this a good number to reach you?" Jackson sounded distracted and Margot picked up on the ambient noise from his end of the call. He'd either moved somewhere that had more noise, or he was trying to obscure the nature of the call.

"Yes."

"Your email on file is still active?"

"It is. Sir, please know that I'm not asking you to do anything illegal or that could jeopardize your career."

"Quade, you're a good soldier and from what I saw, a good Chaplain. You kept our boys' heads on straight over there. It's not easy losing one of your own and I bear the blame for Abrams' death as much as anyone. I changed up that assignment. So, if Nesbit's got himself in trouble over it, I'm going to do what I can to help him. Keep your eye on your email. I'll be in touch."

Jackson ended the call and Margot set the phone back into the cradle. When she looked up, the door stood ajar and Catalina hovered there. Athena was wriggling in her mother's arms, starting to get fussy.

"Was that who took Derek and Sam?" Catalina's red-rimmed eyes begged Margot for good news.

"No. But it might be someone who can help."

"What do you mean?"

"Look, let me see if this brings any useful information. If it does, we'll go to the police together." Margot dug her keys out of her pants pocket. "I moved into the parsonage a while back. Please, go and get a little rest. Focus on Athena and keep her calm. The second I hear anything, I'll let you know."

Catalina accepted the keys. "Thank you."

Now, Margot had to be patient enough to let Jackson dig into Peter's file. As she settled back into her chair, she latched on to something Jackson had said. It had been his decision to change the driving detail that day.

She closed her eyes, trying to recall every detail of that horrible day. Her phone buzzed, interrupting her thoughts with a new incoming message.

The same unknown number was on the screen. She steeled herself for whatever had come in.

The message was unaccompanied by any image and simply said, *He's running out of time. Hate having to give him his last rites, again.*

5

She knew she should report the newest contact to the police and let them try to trace the phone, but the message was clear. She was running short on time and she still had no idea who was behind this.

Against her better judgement, Margot responded to the message. *What do you want from me?*

She waited for any reply, but none came. Either the kidnapper hadn't yet seen the message, or they weren't going to respond. It had been worth a try. She stayed by the phone in her office just in case Jackson called her back. It gave her time to contemplate what had led to the current situation. The circumstances leading up to the IED and the direct aftermath had been burned into her brain.

"No hard feelings about the switch-up, right D?" Peter said with that trademark smile.

"'Course not, Petey. Besides, we both know you could drive circles around me and everyone else here," Derek answered. *He turned to Margot.* *"I still can't believe Jack took me off driving duty for having one drink."*

"I'm not going to judge you," Margot said, *"but he did give a direct order to everyone in the unit to stay out of the mess hall. You disobeyed."*

"I know. And it won't happen again, but it just seems kind of petty. Besides, it's not like I'm hung over."

Margot raised her eyebrows and in a maternal tone said. "Derek, accept your punishment and learn from it. Besides, haven't you been the one talking about how Peter needs some more experience?"

"I know." Derek climbed into the back of the Humvee and offered Margot a hand to get into the vehicle.

They pulled out and headed over the desert terrain. Wind whipped against the tiny windshield, sending showers of sand into their path. Peter bent down to fiddle with the control for the windshield wipers when the first jolt of the chassis hitting something hard shook the vehicle.

"What was that?" Derek called up to Peter.

"No idea, maybe a rock?" Peter's voice was drowned out by the sudden eruption around them of heat and flame.

The phone rang on the desk, jarring Margot from the memory. She scrambled for the receiver, pressing it to her ear. "Hello?"

"Chaplain, it's Jackson."

Margot blinked. The clock on the computer indicated she'd only spoken to him maybe twenty minutes ago. "Did you find something?"

"Not much. Just that the report was made to his parents. Looks like he has a brother named John."

"He never mentioned a brother."

"The brother's in Army Intelligence. Records are sealed. That's all I got, not that any of this sounds particularly useful."

"I wouldn't be so sure about that," Margot answered. "Thanks for the help."

She hung up the phone and stared at the clock on the computer screen. Why had Peter never mentioned a brother in the military? He'd specifically said that he'd been the first in his family to enlist. Had his brother joined after his death? Given the nature of military intelligence, she wasn't likely to find much in terms of John Abrams' service record. Although there were other ways she could find information.

Pulling up a web browser, she logged into

Facebook and found Peter's page. It obviously hadn't been updated in years, but still people shared memories and birthday messages, even after his passing. She'd friended him while they were still deployed, so she had access to his earlier posts and a list of his friends. She started at the very beginning of his profile, when he joined at the age of fourteen. She scrolled through photos of him and high school friends. In every single one, he was beaming and being the joker. She had no doubt he'd been the class clown in school, too.

"Come on, give me something," she pleaded while continuing to sift through pictures.

Finally, she found one slew of birthday wishes from three years ago, when he'd turned eighteen. A woman, who based on the comments to the post was his mother, had posted two photos. One showed two small infants and the second pictured two boys in matching graduation regalia. With identical looks of embarrassment on their faces.

"Oh, God." Despite spending months with him, she couldn't tell Peter from this other boy. It suddenly made perfect sense why Derek would have thought he saw Peter. He and John were twins.

Margot abandoned the church office and sprinted back toward the police station. She was halfway there when a car pulled up beside her.

Veronica Morris-Sawyer rolled down the window and looked over at her. "Is everything okay? I was trying to catch up with you to get some quotes for the paper, but you took off before I could find you."

"Now isn't really a good time. I'm sorry. I'm in the middle of something."

Veronica pulled the car to a stop and leaned over to open the passenger side door from the inside. "Get in. This town isn't that big, but it's still big enough that walking takes longer than driving."

Margot accepted the ride, belting in before Veronica put the car in gear and started forward. "So where are we heading?"

"The police station."

"What's going on? I know the look of someone distressed. I covered the Conrad Baptiste case, remember. You see a lot of desperation when a family member is missing. You may be good at keeping your emotions in check, Reverend, but I know that look now. Please, how can I help?'

"Sam and Derek Nesbit have been abducted, and I think I know who did it. But I need to fill the chief in."

"Abducted? How? Where?"

"There was one weak point in the parade route. And it looks like whoever took them was able to convince Derek he knew the attacker."

"God, I'm so sorry."

"We don't have a lot of time to figure it all out. I'm beginning to understand what motivated the abductor. Still it doesn't explain everything."

"Does whatever led to Derek's abduction have something to do with Sam? Wasn't she the responding officer on his uncle's death?"

"I don't think this has anything to do with Sam. She was collateral damage. Just in the wrong place at the wrong time. Although that doesn't mean the kidnapper won't hurt Sam if they are pushed too far. For now at least they won't hurt my cousin, because they can use her as leverage."

They pulled into the station parking lot and Margot gave Veronica a grateful look. "Thanks for the ride. I promise when everything is done, with Derek and Sam home safe, I'll give you the exclusive story."

"You don't have to do that. I'd much rather report on the parade and how it brought the town together. This place deserves some happy news now and again. Don't you think?"

"I do."

Margot undid the seatbelt and climbed out of the car. She didn't get further than beyond the curb at the front door before the chief appeared.

He said, "We need to talk."

"Yes, we do."

"There's been another message, this time to the police. Whoever took Derek and Sam wants you."

"I know. I think I might know who's behind the abduction. Peter had a twin brother named John in military intelligence. I would imagine that losing his brother in combat would be stressful."

"Enough to kidnap a law enforcement officer and fellow officer to try and hurt them?"

"We have no idea about his mental state. Still, given the right circumstances, I'd say absolutely. So yes, let me go and talk to him."

"You aren't in the service anymore, Reverend. You don't have to put your life on the line. If we tried to take precautions like a body camera or listening device, there's a chance he'd find them and you'd be going in without backup."

"Sir, I know I may look it, but I'm not a civilian. I have had training," Margot protested.

"The same training as the man holding one of my best officers and a friend of yours against their will," the chief retorted.

"I can talk to him. If anything, he probably wants answers about what happened. The army wouldn't have told him anything in detail other than his brother was killed in action. He's grieving. Let me try to help him."

"Only you would see some lunatic as being in need of saving, Reverend."

"Everyone deserves a chance at redemption. He hasn't done something he can't walk away from."

"Yet."

"Where did he want me to go?"

The chief handed over a piece of paper with an address scribbled on it. The zip code was outside of Port Marie. "From what we can tell, it's an abandoned building. Used to be a distillery before it closed up shop."

"Wait, this is outside of town boundaries. You'd have no jurisdiction, right?"

"You let me worry about the red tape. If you're really intent on doing this, we're going with you. I promise that we'll stay out of sight. I'm guessing this guy can spot a wall of blue a mile off."

"Then let's get moving, Sir. Lives are on the line."

6

Margot's heart hammered in her chest as she sat in the backseat of the chief's SUV. He'd opted to take a less conspicuous police vehicle, keeping the lights and sirens off.

"It's just up there about half a block," he told her while easing the vehicle to a stop.

Margot checked her phone to ensure they hadn't missed any more messages from John. He'd gone silent once he'd conveyed his demands to the police.

Margot looked over at the chief. "I know

this is against protocol and you don't like the idea of me going in alone. Honestly, I'm not really fond of it either. Still it's our best shot at bringing everyone out of this alive."

"Rev, you've talked more people into coming clean for what they've done than I've ever seen. People trust you. You inspire something in them. If you can do that with this man, you can do it with anyone. Good luck."

Margot stepped out of the car and pulled her uniform jacket tight around her torso to ward off the chill settling into her bones. Not all small towns were like Port Marie, able to thrive in the face of adversity. Some died out when people moved away to find better lives, doubtless that was what had happened here in Wickerton. She approached the old distillery from the front, hands out so that anyone watching her approach would see she was unarmed. She hadn't carried a weapon since her time overseas and didn't miss it. The weight of it had always been more than a physical burden.

"That's far enough," a male voice called from one of the side windows.

Margot turned to face the speaker, hands held loosely at her sides. "John, can we talk about what you're going through? I want to help you."

"Oh, we'll talk. Open your coat!"

"I'm not armed, John. But if it makes you feel more secure, I'll show you." Margot unbuttoned her jacket, held it open despite the cold, and turned to lift the tails up so he could see she was unarmed.

"Toss your phone. I know your police friends are watching. So, toss it," he ordered.

"You were the one who involved them, John. I asked you what you wanted. You could have told me you wanted to talk with me alone. I would have come straight here."

She got no response. So, she waited, hoping he'd at least let her button up her jacket. After a long thirty seconds he yelled, "Walk toward the door slowly."

Margot did as she was instructed, approaching the door with its missing panes of glass. As she stepped within arm's reach, she saw the tiny red dot of a laser sight on her chest. "I'm just going to open the door, John. That's all."

The dot wavered before disappearing. At least she was gaining his trust.

The door squealed on unused hinges as she forced it to move inward. It scraped along the floor, leaving an arc in the grit and grime. She paused, trying to track any movement within the building that would tell her where John had gone, but there was nothing. She took two steps forward and felt rough hands grab her by the shoulders and yank her sideways.

Margot staggered into a dimly lit room filled with old equipment. Sam lay tied to a pipe, her head lolling to one side in her unconsciousness. Margot couldn't be sure, but she thought she saw shallow breaths moving her cousin's chest up and down.

"She's alive," John's voice said from behind her.

"That's good, John. You haven't done anything drastic."

"Stop saying my name," he spat.

"I can address you by your title if you'd tell me what it is. Military Intelligence is a very good assignment, especially for someone so young."

"You think I'm too stupid to be where I am?"

"On the contrary, I think you'd have to be extremely intelligent to make it there in only a few years. So, please, I'd like to address you by your title. Can you tell me what it is?"

"Lieutenant," he answered.

"Lieutenant Abrams, I want to help you. I want to understand what brought us here today."

John let out a bark of laughter. "Funny, so do I. And your friend here hasn't been very forthcoming."

Margot turned her attention to Derek. He was covered in a thick sheen of sweat. It pooled at his armpits and drenched his shirt. His gaze was unfocused and his cheeks were flushed.

"What did you do to him?" Margot took a step in Derek's direction, but stopped when John's rifle centered on her chest again.

"Only what he did on his own before. Isn't that right, Private Nesbit?"

Derek's lips parted, but he couldn't speak. A jug sat beside him, almost empty, along with a tube and a funnel. John had force-fed him the contents. Given their location, it wasn't hard to determine what the contents had been. Tears stung Margot's eyes as she looked at her friend, in the throes of alcohol poisoning.

"John, Derek had one drink the night before the mission. That was all."

"That's what he said he had. But he was lying."

"No, he wasn't. I was with him that night. I told him not to do it, but he didn't listen. John, that wouldn't have changed things though. We still would have run over that IED. We still would have lost lives."

"But my brother wouldn't have been one of them!"

"I know losing someone you love is difficult. Believe me, I understand. Still lashing out and hurting other people isn't going to absolve you of your grief or your pain. Please, let these people go."

"No. Not until you both know what it's like. He wasn't just my brother. I felt him thousands of miles away. I felt him go."

"I'm so very sorry you had to go through that." Margot shuffled half a step to her left.

"You don't get to be sorry. You just let him die. You didn't do anything."

"I held his hand and I prayed with him. I comforted him in his last moments. I carry that with me every single day. There isn't a day that goes by I don't think about Peter. Yes, he was too young to die, but we don't always understand God's plan. You enlisted after he passed, didn't you?"

"So?"

"So, his death led you to serve your country. You were honoring his memory and his sacrifice by taking up the cause he loved with all his heart."

"No. I didn't. I enlisted so I could find out the truth about what happened to him. You all painted it like it was an accident, but you're all at fault. All of you. Him and the commander. She said …"

"Who said, Lieutenant?"

"Shut up!" John began pacing, the weapon at his side.

If Margot was fast enough, she might be able to get to Sam. Although there was no way she could keep John distracted long enough to free her cousin and Derek from their bonds, let alone get them out of the building safely.

"Go sit over there," John barked, gesturing to a pipe beside Sam. "And tie yourself to the pipe."

"Okay. If that will make you more comfortable," Margot answered and settled by the pipe. She slid the zip ties around her wrists, but didn't tighten them as much as John would have liked. She turned her body to shield her voice as she leaned down to whisper in Sam's ear. "Can you hear me?"

Sam gave a low moan and she opened one eye. It was bloodshot and she seemed to have difficulty focusing on Margot, but Sam was definitely awake.

"I'm going to get you out of here," Margot whispered. "I promise."

7

Margot had no idea how she planned to get Derek and Sam out of the current situation, but she knew she had to try. John kept pacing with the rifle pointed at the floor, muttering to himself. Margot's heart truly broke for his loss, but she also feared what he was capable of, given his mental state. She still didn't know how he knew about the blind spot in the security at the parade.

He'd let slip that 'she' had told him something. He must have had an accomplice. Margot's stomach dropped at the possibility that someone else in town had helped him orchestrate all of this. She didn't think anyone else in town knew Peter or his family. As callous as it sounded, no one in Port Marie aside from Margot and Derek would have cared about John's suffering.

Beside her, Sam moaned and pressed her weight against Margot's hip.

"Who is this guy?" Sam's voice was surprisingly strong given how drugged she appeared.

"How long have you been conscious?" Margot whispered.

"I've been fading in and out for a while. Not sure how long. Whatever he gave me didn't knock me out like he thought it would. He's nuts. He forced Derek to drink pure alcohol. If Derek doesn't get to a hospital soon and get his stomach pumped, he's not going to make it."

"I'm afraid that might be the plan for all of us," Margot answered.

John seemed distracted, preoccupied by something outside the windows. Their whispers carried though and he spun to face them.

"Shut up!" he howled, the rifle swiveling between them.

"You're in charge. Whatever you want," Margot answered, holding up her bound hands in what she hoped was a placating gesture.

He rubbed at his neck with his free hand and moved to the window, peering out, still looking for whatever was pulling his attention.

"What does he want?" Sam hissed, ignoring John's order to be quiet.

"His brother back. Which is impossible since he died in combat in my arms."

"Oh Lord, Margot."

"Tell me what happened? How'd you end up

here?" Margot insisted, her gaze flitting between her cousin and John's pacing form. If Sam could explain quickly enough to fill in the blanks, before John noticed their discussion again, they could start forming a plan of escape.

"I was still worried about the blind spot," Sam said, "so I stationed myself there. Everything seemed fine, even as the participants started coming through. I saw you march by and then I noticed Derek fall out of formation. He took off into the crowd. It seemed weird, so I followed him."

"Then you got caught up in this mess. They weren't ever after you."

"He seemed to know we were related, because he kept saying something about wanting you to know what it felt like. I guess I understand it now."

"I'm so sorry," Margot said.

"You did nothing wrong."

John still remained focused on something

beyond the confines of the distillery. Margot hoped that the chief hadn't sent any uniformed officers in closer. It would mean a death sentence for all of them. John retreated into the hallway, still talking to himself, and Margot exhaled.

"It's eerie, seeing him," she murmured. "He looks exactly like Peter. I still can't wrap my head around the fact that he never mentioned having a twin brother."

"Given how he's acting, I get the feeling maybe Peter was ashamed," Sam answered and tugged on the zip ties around her wrists. The skin beneath the bonds was red and angry. She'd been working at the binds for some time.

"He's grieving and he wants someone to blame, because having a name or a face is easier than accepting that his brother died serving the country he loved. We all knew it was a possibility when we signed up. Of course, none of us ever expect it to be a reality."

"How do you do that?" Sam whispered.

"Do what?" Margot frowned, tugging on her own binds. She'd made them purposefully loose in a bid to escape.

"See the goodness even in the most despicable people? This man is literally trying to murder us and you're trying to help him conquer his grief?"

"Because I don't believe people are born evil. They're made … if that's the case, they can be unmade, too."

"Yeah, but there's still such a thing as self-preservation," Sam argued.

Margot slipped her wrists free of the zip ties that had been keeping her connected to the pipe. "Which is why I didn't tighten those down as much as he probably thought I had." Margot flashed her cousin a smile before darting across the room to check on Derek.

His cheeks were pale and his entire body

shone with a thick layer of sweat. His chest was rising and falling in shallow, ragged movements.

"Hang in there, Derek. We're going to get you out of here," Margot said in his ear.

His head lolled to one side at the sound of her voice. She wasn't sure he'd heard her words or whether he could even understand them since his body was close to shutting down for good. She brushed hair out of his face and tried to lift his weight off the ground. She'd been out of her training regimen for too long. His weight shouldn't have been difficult for her to manage, yet she struggled to get him to his feet.

The upward momentum was enough to trigger Derek's gag reflex and his body did what it could to expel the poison coursing through him. Margot heard a door somewhere in the building slam, but when no footsteps followed it, she assumed that John had gone outside. He had far too much confidence, thinking that he had subdued his hostages.

Margot waited until Derek had stopped dry heaving before searching his uniform for anything, she might use to free Sam's zip ties.

"Don't bother, he took anything useful," Sam said, sensing Margot's train of thought.

"Not everything," Margot answered as she eyed the floor. She eased Derek back down and tugged one of his boot laces free. "I'm going to come right back," she whispered in Derek's ear before returning to Sam's side, holding the lace aloft.

"Please tell me they taught you that in the military," Sam hissed as Margot slipped the lace between her wrist and the plastic of the zip tie. She tugged the lace back and forth rapidly against the plastic and the edges began to fray.

"Nope, YouTube."

"Thank God for DIY videos," Sam sighed as the zip tie came free with a *snick*.

"Help me get him up. We need to get out of here before John comes back," Margot said.

They were halfway across the room to Derek when John loomed large in the doorway. He wasn't alone.

"Where do you think you're going?" Laura stepped up beside John, lacing her fingers into his.

8

Margot stood frozen in the middle of the room, staring in bewilderment at the councilwoman. It should have been obvious to Margot from the moment she'd started asking questions after Derek and Sam went missing. Somehow Margot had been blinded by her belief that people were innately good at their core.

"Why are you doing this?" She finally asked, addressing Laura.

"It's not personal, Reverend. At least not for me. But for John, it's deeply personal."

"You know what he's intending to do, don't you?" Sam asked in an angry voice. "He's going to kill us. You have to know that you'll at the very least be considered an accessory."

Laura merely shrugged in response and took John's rifle, aiming it squarely at Margot's chest. "It's time you back up and tie yourself to that pole properly this time."

"Please, you can't possibly want more lives to be lost," Margot said, her voice firm and pleading. Still, her flight or fight response sent shivers down her spine and her mouth went dry.

"War is cruel, isn't it? It takes people who should have lived and gives a pass to those who shouldn't keep breathing," Laura answered.

Does she really think Derek and I didn't deserve to survive? She doesn't even know us.

Then again, Margot didn't really know Laura either.

"Death is always unfair, Laura. Still it is a part of living. It's what makes our actions on this planet worthwhile. Peter knew that. It's why he signed up to join the Army. He wanted his life to have meaning to others. He wanted to serve." Margot turned her attention back to John. "Believe me, there isn't a day that goes by that I don't think about that loss. You may have felt his passing from thousands of miles away, but I watched the light go out of his eyes. I held him as he cried for comfort, because that was I all I could do. I live with that pain every day." Tears came unbidden and turned her cheeks damp.

"He was my brother," John said. His face had turned red with anger.

"He was our brother, too. You aren't alone in your loss," Margot said as calmly as she could.

"No, you don't get to claim your grief is

the same as his," Laura interrupted, waving the weapon around. The barrel oscillated between Sam, Margot, and a still very incapacitated Derek.

"Laura, look at me." Margot stepped forward. She caught Sam shaking her head out of the corner of her eye.

"Shut up!" Laura shouted.

"You are clearly hurting. If you see no other choice than to hurt us, can't you do us the courtesy of at least explaining what we've done to you ... to deserve this?"

"Weren't you listening?" she said. "It's not about you."

"No, but it's about someone. Who did you lose?" Margot shuffled forward again. She said a silent prayer that the police had decided she'd been gone far too long and were on their way to take the building. "Please, I'd like to know."

Laura shook her head, tears streaming down her cheeks. Margot thought back to what she knew about the woman. Until the parade planning, Margot hadn't had much interaction with Laura. She wasn't a member of any of the faith communities.

Laura finally said, "Commander Flannery is the reason my husband, Tyler, is gone. He's the real problem. Don't worry, he'll get what's coming to him."

"I know Jackson Flannery," Margot said. "He's a good man. He made the decision to take Derek off driving duty that day, because he didn't want a potentially impaired driver operating the Humvee. That was the responsible thing to do."

"He chose wrong," John growled.

"I know that nothing I say is going to change how you feel. But, please, consider what you are doing. You have to know that this ends in either you two going to jail, or bringing even more grief to your families, because they will have to bury you. The police are looking for Derek and Sam. You contacted them yourself, remember? You told them to send me." Margot inched forward again. She was almost in reach of the rifle's muzzle.

"I told them not to come anywhere near here," John spat.

"So far they have respected your wishes. We've done everything you've asked, John. Your issue is with Derek and me. Let Sam go. She isn't part of our loss. You want to punish those you deem responsible; Sam wasn't overseas. This isn't about her."

"She should have stayed out of it, then," Laura answered. "She should have just done her job and minded her own business."

"Investigating suspicious things is what I do, Laura," Sam interjected. She hadn't moved, which surprised Margot. Margot had hoped her cousin would have at the very least flanked her so they could try to subdue John and Laura simultaneously.

"Have you talked to someone about your

loss? A counselor?" Margot redirected the conversation back to Laura.

"Where do you think we met?" Laura said. "A support group for the family members of soldiers killed in action."

"Do you think the other members of your group would condone what you two are doing?"

"They're weak and too afraid to take the action that needed to be done."

This situation wasn't going to be resolved until someone took action. Margot reached forward and grabbed the barrel of the rifle, struggling to get it free from Laura's grasp. The other woman tugged hard against Margot's grip, but neither relinquished the weapon.

Instead, Laura's finger found the trigger.

She squeezed off a shot. The bullet ricocheted off the ceiling, striking an old pipe. Both women stopped and stared in momentary horror as a massive fireball erupted, feeding off the old wood and machinery parts of the distillery.

"We need to get out of here, now!" Margot yelled as pieces of the room began raining down on them.

9

Ceiling beams crumbled above their heads as Margot wrenched the rifle out of Laura's hands. They both staggered backward, narrowly avoiding a plummeting beam that crashed to the cement floor between them. The fire that had erupted when the bullet struck the pipe continued to consume everything nearby, which would include Derek if she didn't act quickly.

Tossing the weapon out of Laura's reach, Margot raced to her friend's side.

"Sam, help me!" Margot shouted above the blaze.

No reply.

She turned in the direction her cousin had been, but the smoke was filling in too quickly and she couldn't see if Sam was okay. Margot had to believe that Sam could take care of herself. So, she focused her attention on Derek instead. "Hang in there, soldier. I've got you."

Margot hefted Derek's weight onto her shoulders. Somehow, despite the lack of training and the difficulty she'd had earlier in lifting him, she was able to bear his weight. Smoke continued to fill the structure, choking the air out of Margot's lungs. Her vision started to blur at the periphery. Derek's chest still rose and fell in shallow bursts. *Please Lord, see us through this.* She moved in the direction she assumed the exit to be.

A figure loomed in the smoke and collided with her, sending her toppling backward. Her head smacked hard against the concrete and stars flashed in her dwindling vision. Before she could move, thick hands wrapped around her throat and squeezed. Every instinct in her body told her to fight back, but she did her best to make her body go limp. If her attacker believed they'd succeeded in suffocating her, she had a chance to make it out of the building alive. One of the hands released and slammed a fist into the side of her head.

Pain radiated through her jaw. It continued up through the back of her neck and around her left ear. Still, she remained silent. The crackling of wood being turned into kindling faded as did the brightness of the blaze around them. Finally, her assailant left her for dead, staggering away.

Margot lay motionless on the floor, failing to summon the will to move. The pain had turned to numbness. She knew, in some part of her brain, that the numbness was a bad sign. She could almost stay there and let the Lord take the reins. If this was her time, then she would not fight Him.

A face flashed above her through the haze as her throat fought to pull in air. Peter's face hovered near her.

"Get up, Chaplain. This fight isn't over yet. This isn't your time," she heard the words in her mind.

She focused all of her energy on taking a breath, welcoming the ache in her throat and chest at the effort. It meant she was still alive. She rolled to her right and forced herself onto her hands and knees. The motion was enough to upset her stomach, but she held back the bile until the nausea passed.

"Derek?" She croaked. Her voice was barely loud enough to be heard over the blaze.

She crawled back the way she thought Derek must have fallen. Margot groped along the grimy floor until she felt the bend of an elbow. Not considering it could be one of her captors, she latched on and began to drag the motionless figure toward the exit. Margot's belly crossed the threshold into the hallway and the floor grew cooler beneath her. The air was a little easier to breathe.

"Fire department, call out!" A deep bass voice boomed off to her left.

This isn't our time. Peter was right.

"Here," she called, raising an arm to signal their location.

A man appeared above her in turnout gear and an oxygen mask. She couldn't identify him, although Port Marie's fire department was relatively small.

"I've got two by the front entrance," the man said into the radio on his shoulder before bending to offer Margot a hand.

"Take him first; he needs a hospital. Please." She shoved Derek into the firefighter's embrace.

"Can you walk?" He hoisted Derek onto his shoulder.

Can I? Margot scrambled to her feet, swaying slightly as she took in the smokier air.

"Stay close," he ordered.

She grabbed a fistful of his jacket and let him lead her out of the building where ambulances waited. Margot released her grip on the firefighter and turned to look at the distillery, now engulfed in flames. Other rescue workers manned hoses, fighting the blaze from the street. It appeared she and Derek were the first to be pulled from the fire. *Sam's still inside!*

"I need to go back in there," Margot announced, starting forward.

"Miss, you need to get checked by the paramedics," a different firefighter told her, pulling her back.

"I have family in there," Margot argued.

"Let us do our job. Please, you need to get checked out."

Margot fought the firefighter's iron grip one last time before letting herself be ushered to the second ambulance. The other medics were tending to Derek's injuries, trying to get a breathing tube into his airway.

"He has severe alcohol poisoning. You need to pump his stomach," Margot said as a third medic began washing the cut on Margot's cheek.

"They know what they're doing," the medic tending to her said.

Margot's stomach clenched as she surveyed the scene before her. The longer the first responders took to clear the building, the less likely she would see Sam alive. Flames licked the outside of the structure now. As another fireball punched through the roof, she could swear she heard another gunshot. Tears fell unbidden down her cheeks, mixing with the grime on her face from the smoke.

"Here, this will help you breathe a little easier." The medic slid an oxygen mask over Margot's nose and mouth.

I won't breathe easier until I know Sam is okay.

After an interminable length of time, two firefighters rounded the side of the building carrying a female figure between them. Margot abandoned the oxygen mask as soon as she spotted the gleam of a badge on the woman's chest.

"Sam!" Margot skidded in the dirt and grasped her cousin's hand.

The blood staining Sam's uniform was bright and sticky this close. Margot refused to relinquish her cousin's hand as the fire-fighters took her to another ambulance for treatment.

"She's got a gunshot wound to the lower

left abdomen," one of the firefighters said before turning back to the blaze.

"Give the medics room to work," the other first responder said, guiding Margot back to the middle ambulance.

"She's my cousin. Please, I need to be with her."

"You're all heading to the hospital. You can see her there. You need to focus on yourself right now. Okay?"

A wave of exhaustion came over Margot and she sank to the gurney inside the ambulance. Her head throbbed in time to the sirens wailing overhead and she leaned against the pillow. The medic slipped the oxygen mask back over Margot's face and she let the fresh air clear her lungs. Somehow it was enough to lull her into the relief of sleep.

Margot woke to find herself in a hospital bed. The overhead lights were agonizingly bright to her retinas. She moaned and rubbed at the side of her face. A thick strip of gauze padded her cheek and above her eye. The realization of what had happened spurred her out of bed, much to the dismay of the monitors she pulled off in her bid for freedom. She needed to find Sam and Derek, make sure they'd made it through the ordeal. What had become of Laura and John?

"You need to get back in bed," a nurse in purple scrubs said, meeting Margot at the doorway.

"I came in with two other people—a woman with a gunshot wound and a man suffering from alcohol poisoning. Please, I need to make sure they're okay."

"Nurse, why don't you let me talk to Reverend Quade," Reverend Hawley said, appearing behind the nurse's shoulder.

The nurse stepped into the room to

check Margot's vitals and reattach her to the monitors that were still blaring angrily behind her. The whole time, Margot kept quiet as she waited for the nurse to leave. Reverend Hawley sat in one of the large armchairs beside the window. He studied his hands, which did not instill Margot with confidence.

"Now, until the doctor clears you, don't go for any walkabouts, okay?" The nurse chided before leaving them in peace.

"If you have bad news, please just tell me," Margot said.

"I do have news." He wouldn't meet her gaze.

"Please, Patrick, just tell me."

He exhaled a long breath and leaned forward, hands on his knees. "Sam is in surgery still, but they think she's going to make it."

"Thank the Lord. And Derek?"

He bowed his head. "His body shut down ... there was too much damage from his condition—had gone on for too long. He was pronounced dead on arrival. His wife and daughter were able to say goodbye to him."

A sob ripped from Margot's chest and she slid down in the hospital bed, curling into herself. John and Laura had accomplished what they'd set out to do after all. Anger bubbled in her throat, hot and acidic. She did her best to swallow it back. There was a time for anger and this was definitely not it. She would have plenty of chances to properly grieve this new loss. She tried to focus on the fact that Sam was going to pull through.

Reverend Hawley ended the call and reached out to squeeze Margot's hand. "I'm so very sorry for your loss, Margot. Derek was a kind soul and a good man."

She accepted his gesture of support and held tight for a few seconds as she tried to compose herself.

"I can't imagine what is going through your mind right now, Margot. Can you tell me how it all happened? Last I knew, there was some sort of security breach and the next thing I hear; they've brought back people injured in an explosion."

Margot took a couple of steadying breaths and forced herself to look at her mentor and friend. "Back when Derek Nesbit and I were serving overseas, we lost a brother in arms. His name was Peter Abrams. He died when we hit an IED. We never knew he had a brother named John. An identical twin brother. It turns out, John was more than a little grief-stricken by his loss. He blamed us and our commanding officer for his brother's death. It appears he met Laura Finch in a veteran's grief support group. She blames our commanding officer for the death of her husband."

"I'm so sorry you had to bear that burden yourselves."

Margot tugged the blankets up over her torso in a bid to ward off the chill settling over her. "I thought I'd gotten to a point that I was at least able to handle Peter's death. But we need to warn Commander Flannery that he may be in danger. Please, he's stationed in Georgia."

"Of course." Reverend Hawley produced a cell phone from his pocket and dialed, putting the call on speaker phone. "Chief, it's Patrick Hawley. I'm with Margot Quade. She says her commanding officer is danger."

"His name is Jackson Flannery. He's stationed down in Georgia right now. Please, you need to get word to the military police that someone is targeting him." The words tumbled out of Margot's mouth so fast she wasn't sure that they were coherent.

"We're on it," the chief answered over the line.

Margot wiped fresh tears off her bandaged cheek. "Derek didn't deserve to die like that. Although, if this was his time, then I can't argue with the Lord."

"Margot, sometimes people die and it's not God's plan. Sometimes it is just human cruelty."

She shook her head. "I refuse to believe that. These people were grieving and they let that grief control them. It made them lash out at anyone they blamed."

Reverend Hawley sat back in the chair and said nothing. They shared the silence for a while longer until heavy footfalls echoed in the hallway, rousing Margot enough to see the police chief standing in the doorway.

"Is now a good time?" His voice was soft and she could tell he'd shed tears of his own recently.

"Of course. Please come in, Chief," Margot answered.

He crossed the threshold and gave Reverend Hawley a nod and said nothing when the former did not vacate his chair. The chief turned his attention to Margot. "Officer Raymond is out of surgery and headed up to recovery. She'll be in ICU for a little while, but once they get her settled, I think she'd like to see you."

"I'd like that very much. Thank you."

"Mind if I ask a few questions about what happened?"

"Right. I'll need to file another statement."

"Not right now. I just need to know how things ended up in a fiery blaze with multiple fatalities."

"John and Laura didn't make it?"

"No. They both succumbed to smoke inhalation."

"Sam and I warned them that this might result in their deaths as well," Margot muttered.

"What was their motivation, for doing this? I mean, I could understand John Abrams. You said as much before we let you go in to try and talk him down. Why Laura Finch?"

"She lost her husband overseas, under the

direction of our commanding officer. John and Laura met at a grief support group and decided to take matters into their own hands. From what I gathered upon arriving, they'd forced Derek to drink pure grain alcohol. It was shutting his body down before I even arrived."

"That is never a call I ever want to make. Having to tell a family we've failed to save their loved one." The chief sighed.

"I was trying to talk Laura down and get the rifle away from her when it went off." Margot closed her eyes, trying to hold in her grief. "It hit a pipe with flammable materials and the whole building went up in flames. That's all I know. I remember hearing a second gunshot after I made it outside, and then I saw two firefighters carrying Sam out."

"Thank you for your statement, Reverend. Get some rest. I'll let you know when Sam is accepting visitors. And I thought you'd like to know we contacted Jackson Flannery. He's safe."

SAM REMAINED in the hospital for another three days before being discharged. Margot had spent most of it at her bedside as she slept and regained her strength. On the second day, as Margot sat by her cousin's bedside, head bowed in prayer, Sam had rolled over and mumbled something under her breath.

"What was that?" Margot lifted her head.

"I said it must have been pretty bad if you're sitting there praying like I'm dying."

"Don't joke about that. You nearly didn't make it." Margot's throat closed in on itself before she could add that Derek hadn't.

"After the fire started, everything went kind of crazy," Sam said, struggling to sit up and wincing.

"I know," Margot replied, touching the now smaller bandage on the side of her face.

"I watched you go for Derek and then John came at me. I thought I could take him out, but the visibility was terrible. He hit me in the head and I blacked out for a while. No idea how long. I lost all track of Laura, but she must have gotten ahold of the gun again and fired off another shot." She pressed her fingers lightly to the wound on her side.

"Neither of them survived," Margot said.

"Is it wrong of me to say I'm glad?"

"I think maybe you were right to be skeptical of some people. Maybe they don't all have good in them. Besides, they got what they wanted—my suffering. Derek succumbed to the alcohol poisoning and smoke inhalation."

"No, Margot, that can't be right."

Margot nodded, fresh tears making her vision misty. "I told Catalina I'd do everything I could to bring her husband back … I failed."

"None of this is on you. Those two were playing games the whole time. They could have lured you in a lot sooner than they did. His death is on their hands."

"I just can't believe he's gone. It's been two days and still I don't quite believe it. I watched Peter take his last breath. That image is forever seared into my mind. Still I never got to say goodbye to Derek."

"If it helps, he went out like a true soldier and a hero."

"What do you mean?" Margot forced herself to sit up straight and wiped the tears away.

"John was going to make me drink the alcohol, but Derek insisted it be him. He kept telling me that he had to atone for something he'd done overseas. I begged him to stop drinking after the first bottle, but John wouldn't let him stop. Derek said it was okay. He was doing it to set things right and even the scales. I didn't realize what he meant until you told me who John was."

"He saved you," Margot said.

Sam nodded. "He did, even knowing he might not make it. You were right, no one wants to die. But sometimes, to protect other people and loved ones, they choose to make that sacrifice. So please, Margot, don't take this blame and guilt on yourself. You've carried enough blame for something that was entirely out of your control for far too long. Don't let Derek's death be the start of a new cycle of blame and hate."

nlike the other tragedies that had befallen Port Marie in the preceding two years, the loss of Derek Nesbit hit the town hard. Perhaps they, too, had felt the betrayal of one of their own council members taking matters into their own hands. Or perhaps they had just all felt sorry to see such a once-prominent family ripped apart yet again by violence.

Margot stood at the front of the sanctuary, staring out at the assembled congregation much like she'd done every Sunday, although this time was after an extended break. Just like the time after her ordeal with the Arthurs, Reverend Hawley had stepped in while she healed from her injuries.

Sam sat in the front row of pews with a crutch propped beside her. Her bullet wound was well on the mend. She had a long road of physical therapy ahead of her, but she was going to survive and even return to her position on the police force.

Veronica had written a small piece on what had happened, beautifully framing the narrative around honoring the sacrifices of the men and women of the military.

People still crammed into the room, resorting to bringing in extra folding chairs or standing along the outer walls. Derek's memorial service had been just as packed, bringing Catalina to tears. The judge who'd overseen Mary Nesbit's case had granted her a one-day pass to attend her nephew's funeral. Margot had expected Mary to be angry with Margot, to blame her. Instead, she'd been frail and withdrawn. They'd barely spoken as two guards ushered her back to a waiting van at the end of the service. She had been given leave to say goodbye to to her great niece, and that was it. Catalina had even tried to speak to Mary, to share a moment of grief, but the guards had refused to let her even near Mary.

For her part, Catalina hadn't blamed Margot for failing to save her husband. When she'd learned what Derek had done, she'd put on a sad smile. She said that she expected nothing less from the man she loved.

At present, Margot tried to find familiar faces amongst the sea of people. She hadn't anticipated so many coming on her first Sunday back.

Reverend Hawley snuck up the steps to

the pulpit and patted her on the shoulder. "You look nervous. I've never seen you nervous before a sermon."

"This feels different. It's like the end of a long story, somehow. Besides it isn't an ending I'd ever anticipated or wanted."

"God works in ways we can't always understand or anticipate. You know that, but you and Sam were brought through this tragedy for a reason."

"But we lost another brother-in-arms along the way. It's a loss that shouldn't have happened."

"No, it shouldn't have, but Derek took a risk. He knew he might not come back from it in order to protect others. That was his nature. Shouldn't we reflect on that and honor that bravery?"

Margot turned her back to the congregation and clasped her hands in front of her. "I am trying every day to remember that. I always believed that people deserve a second chance when they've done wrong, because so often circumstances beyond their control had such a profound impact on their actions. However now, after seeing what grief and anger led John and Laura to do, I waver in that belief, Patrick."

"You need to tell the congregation that. They've all come to hear your words of wisdom. Be honest and straight with them. They are your community. Your brothers and sisters in arms. They will lift you up and support you as you navigate what you're feeling." He reached behind her and took her sermon notes. "Forget whatever you had planned for today. This is about your healing, now."

Reverend Hawley stepped down from the pulpit, leaving Margot alone to turn and face her congregation. Two years ago, she'd been so unsure about returning home and finding a place here in Port Marie. Derek had been such an integral part of her journey, of making her the person she'd become. She did owe it to his memory to lean on and embrace the people who had welcomed her to lead them spiritually.

"Good morning everyone." She gripped the edges of the lectern as she took a steadying breath. *You can do this. Have faith.* "I arrived this morning with a sermon prepared. But as a good friend reminded me, sometimes you need to just speak from the heart."

A few murmurs and chuckles went up from the gathered crowd and heads craned to look at Reverend Hawley who sat beside Sam in the front row.

Margot focused on her cousin's face. "As most of you know, I lost a very good friend of mine a short time ago, in one of the most painful ways imaginable. I'll be honest with you. I've been struggling to come to terms with what happened to him. Grief comes at me like a wave and sometimes, it's strong enough to pull me under. I've always prided myself on seeing the best in others, because I believe that God would not create his children to harm and tear down one another. But that belief was tested."

Sam sat up straighter in her seat, locking eyes with Margot. She mouthed 'I'm here for you' and Margot couldn't help but smile. Reverend Hawley had been right yet again. The people around her were going to help see her through these trials and buoy her back to where she wanted to be.

"I've been tested," she repeated. "But, here's the thing, I know I'm not alone. I have every single person standing in this room to share the load. Because that's what community is about. We carry the good and the bad together so that no one person has to be weighed down. I lost sight of that after everything that happened with Derek Nesbit's death, but I think I'm beginning to see things more clearly now. So, I hope that in the days and weeks to come, we can all remember to lean on one another when we struggle. I may no longer be serving in the military, but you all are my brothers-in-arms now— meaning we defend and support one another until the end."

The sea of smiling faces made Margot's chest swell with hope. A sense of peace settled over her like a favorite blanket, reminding her that it is there to comfort her. It would take time to fully heal from these wounds, but she no longer doubted that she could. *I have faith and that is enough.*

Ready for more mysteries? Grab Pains and

Penalties, and join Kalina Greystone for a brand new series!

Join Sarah's Newsletter for all the latest news!
Subscribe here!

S.E. Biglow is the pen name of *USA Today* bestselling author Sarah Biglow. She lives in Massachusetts with her husband and son. She is a licensed attorney and spends her days combatting employment discrimination as an Investigator with the Massachusetts Commission Against Discrimination.

You can find an up-to-date list of all my books here

www.ingramcontent.com/pod-product-compliance
Lightning Source LLC
Chambersburg PA
CBHW061218190726
48288CB00001B/231